WHAT THE HELL IS WRONG WITH YOU?

BIG DADDY MIKE

NEWMAN SPRINGS PUBLISHING
320 Broad Street
Red Bank, NJ 07701

First originally published by Newman Springs Publishing 2021

ISBN 978-1-63692-992-7 (Paperback)
ISBN 978-1-63692-993-4 (Digital)

Printed in the United States of America

I want to start out by saying that writing this book has been a lot of fun. It is pretty fucked up and nasty, so if you don't like that sort of thing, you should stop reading right now. It was not really planned except for the "WTF" section of this book, as you will see if you actually read it all the way through, like I hope you do. The football sections of this book were not planned and just kind of happened. I was filling in as commissioner for a fantasy league and started giving people shit each week on the blog. People liked it, so I kept doing it each week. Then it just morphed into writing stories about certain people in the league each week (none of them true). I had no idea the effect it had on people and how much it made them laugh until I skipped a week. I got phone calls and emails saying, "WTF."

"Where is your write-up?" one guy told me. "I like to sit out on the deck, read it to my wife while having my morning coffee."

I started reading it to my brother and son to see if what I wrote that week was funny, and after they laughed, I would post it. They always thought it was funny, sometimes funnier than other times. But they always laughed, and I appreciated it.

Each team in the fantasy leagues came up with their own team names. I changed them in the write-ups I did each week to something a little funnier. I did not always call them the same name, but I think you can follow who it was just by what I wrote about each one. I did lose a lot of the stuff I wrote in the early days, which pisses me off. The problem is I don't remember what I wrote, so I can't recreate it. Even as I was going back through this material, I found myself laughing because it was like it was the first time I read it.

The poem section was something I started when I wrote a poem for my son Zaq for his sixteenth birthday. Not sure why, as I am not a poem person, but something told me to write a poem for him for his birthday.

Let's just say right up front that they are not your typical poems and are more of a roast than a poem, but they rhyme, so I call them poems.

Let me explain the layout of the book a little bit.

The list of characters is just a little write-up about each person so you kind of get a feel of who they are.

The first section is a family fantasy football league. There are usually about eight of us.

The second section is a pick'em league that has roughly thirty people from season to season, where we just pick the winners of all the football games. I don't write about everyone in that league, but I try to get most of them at some point but not every week.

The third section is all the poems that I have written. They are pretty fucked up, so read at your own risk.

The fourth section is about the shit that happens to me on a daily basis that I remember to write about. That is, if I think it would be funny to other people. It also has stories about when I was growing up that I thought was funny. It is just a hodgepodge of shit that I think is funny. If this book sells, then I will be writing more. Even if it doesn't, I will probably still write for the family because they find it funny. I like to make people laugh because it brings me joy to see people happy and laughing.

Before you get started reading this book, I would like to thank my brother Doug (GrizzleMcfucknuts) for being such a good sport and actually laughing at the shit I write about him. The one comment he makes each time, which comes to mind, is "What the fuck is wrong with you?" And then he laughs. Also, my son Lane laughs uncontrollably when reading the shit I write about him and Doug. They are my official sounding boards, and I appreciate it.

The other person I would like to thank is Chris. He is the artist that found it in his heart to actually draw what is on the cover. I tried other artists, but when I told them what I wanted, they cut off all communication with me. What a bunch of pussies. They don't mind watching *Fifty Shades of Grey* or taking it in the ass with a frozen cucumber, but ask them to draw a naked cartoon, and they get all righteous on you. I hope the next time these so-called artists are blowing someone, their ball sack leaves a bruise on their chin.

4

FAMILY LEAGUE 2017

List of characters

The Commissioner is fifty-four years old. He is one of the nicest guys you will ever meet. He is probably the funniest guy on the planet (unless you are his wife). He is good-looking, with a full head of hair, and is actually the epitome of physical fitness. He should be on a fireman's calendar and has been asked, but he has turned them down on numerous occasions. Obviously, he is an awesome writer and hung well enough to be making millions in the porn industry but chose a different life. I just can't say enough about this guy. People want to be around him, and some want to be him. He truly is one of a kind and loved by all.

The Griz is fifty-eight years old. He is a big burley guy who looks like a grizzly bear. He has long hair, has a long beard, and wears nothing but tank tops and shorts (even if it is zero degrees outside). He is one of the nicest guys you will ever meet but can be mean as a snake if need be. He has one bad wheel, so he walks with a limp. He has at least one swollen nut and some type of infection near his mud whistle during the season. He likes to hunt Big Game and eat turkey shit out of my yard. He will gladly shit in your garden for a dollar if you ask him to. He likes to travel and suck on belly button lint to pass the time while driving and has been known to shoot lint

5

from his bunghole. I can't say if he has fucked a groundhog, but I have seen a groundhog fuck start his face while he was asleep in his hammock. My question is, Was he really asleep? I have also heard him tell squirrels to go home because they are drunk. Don't know what that's about.

Ramsey is twenty-two years old, skinny, and kind of tall. He has short curly hair, not curly like pubic hair but more than just wavy. He has big ears that stick out from the side of his head; if you are looking at him straight on, it kind of looks like a city cab coming at you with the doors open. He has a little bit of acne. He gets a hard-on every time he sees a shopping cart. Not sure what that's about. It's a bit weird, but he likes to stuff marbles in his ass, go outside naked, and shoot the marbles at squirrels. He has never even come close to hitting one, but he keeps trying. In the fall, the neighbors don't like it too much because there are no leaves on the trees, so they can see him and his ass full of marbles running through the trees and releasing marbles from his stink star at the squirrels. He thinks the Commish is funny, which is true.

Thatsurbaby is forty-six years old. She is the Commissioner's wife. She is a little blond, with a big attitude; mean as a junkyard dog but can be nice also, just don't give her any shit in the morning when she comes around the corner looking like Rod Stewart when he gets his hair ready for a concert. Who yelled and where the fuck did that apple come from? This is an inside joke that if you want to hear about, you can call the Commish, and he will tell you the story.

Lilmama is twenty-seven years old, is a redhead but more of a strawberry blonde, sucks at fantasy football, but is nice to everyone. She thinks it's funny when she says, "Come to Lynchburg, Virginia, if you want your ass kicked."

Genewilder, I think, is around thirty-nine years old and kind of looks like Gene Wilder but is not exactly. He has wild curly hair and is pretty funny. He thinks the Commish is hilarious, so he is okay in the Commish's book. He is very sarcastic, and the Commish loves it.

Asshole Licker is a big old boy, is maybe fifty-eight years old, got a noggin like Shrek, and kind of looks like Homer Simpson. He wears a size 15 shoe, but don't let it fool you. His dick looks like a chocolate chip out of a cookie on account that he keeps it tucked in his ass for when he is performing at the local cabaret. Which would explain his double camel toe or, as I like to call it, the Moose Knuckle.

Steelher Virginity is around thirty-five years old and the son-in-law of the Commish. He is a nice guy and pleasant to be around. Good luck catching him awake and not pissing. It's usually one or the other. His calves are like granite boulders, and he can drive a golf ball to the moon. Well, maybe not all the way to the moon but at least halfway.

LilD'bag is sixteen years old, going on forty. He is pretty good at fantasy football but is more obsessed with being tall. He has a blond afro and looks like Doogie Howser. He could probably use a kick in the balls, and the Commish doesn't mind obliging him for that activity.

INTRODUCTION

I just want to welcome all you losers to the house of clowns. That will be the nicest thing I say all season to you backward, hillbilly, sister-fucking, and chicklet-licking retards.

We have a new member this year, and he goes by the name Asshole. I can vouch for him. He is an asshole. Show no mercy on his Homer Simpson—looking ass. Crush his nuts, and if he is any good, we will invite him to the Hula bowling barbecue at the end of the season. Grizzle Mcfucknuts will have to teach him how to Hulabowl. That is if he can get his tooth off that convenience store gas station crackwhore's titty.

I have been meaning to ask you, Grizzlenuts. I thought crack-whores didn't eat much, so I was wondering why she is always shit-ting behind the church with you. The pastor from the church already called me and said they were putting up an electric fence with a locked gate to keep you and your skank off the property.

I heard you and she had a little incident the other day. That rag head Kerpaul who works at the gas station where she hangs out said she was sitting there the other day just smoking a cigarette, wearing what used to be a white tube top and jean shorts hiked up what is left of her ass. You came by with a bunch of balloons for her. How fucking sweet. He then told me that because she only weighs six-ty-two pounds, the balloons lifted her into the air, and she floated away. Too dumb to let go, I guess. It has been reported that you have been seen lurking around the gas station to see if she makes her way back and that you have been seen crying and sucking your thumb.

Don't worry, crackwhores are like kittens. She will find her way back to you. After all, you have all her spare teeth in a Secret's tin you have had since you were seven years old.

I added some new scoring options, so go take a look at that, and let me know if you have any issues. Not that I give a shit, but I will consider changes if I think they need to be made.

Let's all make sure that Terrance does not get a good team this year. I would hate to see her win another ring.

Glad to see the cupcake whore will be here for the draft in person. That way, we can kick her ass in person for making such tasty treats.

Ramsey, get a fucking job and learn how to win. You had the best team last year and blew it, just like you blew that monkey at the zoo. You are nasty.

That's it for now. Have fun this year, and remember to leave your feelings at the door when you enter the realm of the Commish.

Commish out.

SEASON 1

Well, week 1 is over, and I am happy to say the Commish won both games. It looked a little tight there at the beginning, but my superb coaching skills prevailed, and I won them both. It did feel good to whip the newcomer, who goes by the name Asshole. The bad part is my number 1 pick is out for eight weeks. That is just my fucking luck. Quit laughing, dickheads.

Ramsey, WTF, your team sucked it up like a Dyson vacuum. You were all happy after the draft, thinking you did awesome. Game time made your dick go limp, and you couldn't even get a reach around from the Redskins because they sucked also. Get a job, you bum.

Lil Dbag you were all cocky thinking you were going to win both games, but I guess you learned a lesson. Don't open your mouth unless you are a girl because someone is bound to put a cock in it.

Betty Cocker was starting out like last year, on top of the pile, but you will be deflowered before the season is through.

Ben (Gene Wilder), nice try but not even close. You need to take up chess or writing. You should probably quit hanging out with your dad and that crackwhore. What would your mom think if she knew you had joined them for a shit behind the church?

That's Your Baby, lucky wins this week. If you were playing the Commish, you would have gotten your ass spanked just like you like it—hard and rough. You will go down this season, and I don't mean on a goat.

Asshole, nice try on beating the Commish, but we all know you ain't got the stones to take me down. Probably because you have been hanging out with Chelsey Clinton, looking at plastic surgery magazines to get rid of those ugly mugs. All I got left to say to you is "Fuck off, Asshole, and I hope you lose both games next week."

GrizzleMcfucknuts, here we are again, poised for yet another season of disappointment for you and the chicklet-toothed whore. I see in the local paper that you and she made the front page again. You started another sport called sheet (shit skeet) shooting. Un-fucking-believable. I was dumbfounded when I heard what you two were doing at the public park. Apparently, she was shooting clay pigeons out of her ass, and you were shooting them with a shotgun. The report says every time you stepped on her gut, she shot one out of her ass as you yelled, "Shit!" And then you would shoot it out of the sky. I don't think this will be an Olympic sport since you got arrested for indecent exposure by a crackwhore and discharging a weapon in a public park. I know you were raised better. What the fuck is wrong with you?

Until next week, when you all don't suck so bad.

Commish out.

Another week

Well, another week is in the books, and the Commish stank it up like a sweaty ball sack with some gin mixed in. If you don't know it, it is a very nasty smell. Like make-you-throw-up smell if you were trying to blow me. Anyhow, I think you get the point that my team sucked this week.

Ramsey, WTF are you doing? Get it together, man. I don't want to hear excuses that you had to pick up Grizzlenuts and the whore after they got off the late shift. That is no reason for your team to be as shitty as it is. If you think it will help, then quit giving them rides home at all hours of the night. I am sure she can blow someone to get them a ride home. You need your rest for doing nothing all day except snapping your carrot.

Lil Dbag, you got lucky once again that I had such a shitty week. I was the only team you would have beaten. You might want to stick to basketball and have your MeArs powder your little butt. I heard you were at the Grizzlenuts's house and he covered his belly in whipping cream and put a cherry in his belly button. Then he tied your hands behind your back and made you get the cherry out of his belly button. Why would you agree to that? Grizz, WTF?

Betty Cocker, fuck you!

Gene Wilder, apparently you got a little pissed because I called you Gene Wilder and your team went the fuck off. Stop that shit. I am counting on a win when I play you.

That's Your Baby, you are on a roll, but you will be dethroned.

Asshole Licker, I fear I made a mistake by letting you in the league. You really need to keep your scores down. Whatever you do, don't go by the Grizzlenuts's house during shark week. Grizzlenuts's wife shits her pants while hugging a pillow and watching the shows going on during shark week. It smells really nasty, and sometimes you can taste it. I don't know why she watches them because it scares the shit out of her. It doesn't help that Grizz chases her around the house with the remote-controlled hot-air balloon in the shape of a shark. She's running from room to room with the shit falling out of her pant legs. It really is a sight you don't want to see.

Grizzlemcfucknuts, well, well, well, here we are again. Another week has gone by, and we are all dying to hear what happened in the life of Grizz and his sidekick chicklet-toothed whore. First of all, I think it is a tad bit on the cruel side to chase your wife around the house with a remote-controlled air shark scaring the shit out of her. You know how scared she is of those creatures. I fucking hate sharks also. I heard Ramsey was at your house and was having trouble focusing on reality. I heard you found him in a corner with a penny. He was sticking the penny in the electrical outlet, and every time it shocked him, he said "Get a job, they say." And he just kept doing that until you set your nuts on the back of his neck. I guess the smell of shit and ball sweat mixed together snapped him out of his autistic coma. Good thinking, by the way. I would have never thought of that. Maybe you should quit your job at the toll booth and get a job at the hospital snapping people out of comas. Just a thought. I know you always wanted to get into the medical field. Last thing. Let Brady come up for air once in a while, and don't laugh at him with all that whipping cream on his face. He is a sensitive little guy.

That's it for this week. Tune in next week to see if the Grizz gets another job or goes on welfare.

Commish out.

Another week

Well, another week is in the books for the house of clowns, and I must say I am not happy about how my team is performing. With the injury losses and underperformers, it's like being a one-legged man in an ass-kicking contest (not worth a shit).

Ramsey, I see you finally put some points up on the board. Don't worry. That will last about as long as your job as an electrician. What was it, two days? What I am saying is, don't get used to it because the injury bug is coming your way. And don't be making any excuses next week when you start your losing streak all over again. I hear you may be moving into the Grizz household. What the hell is that all about? Maybe you got your eye on his crackwhore to deflower you or you want a shot at shitting behind the church. Anyway, get your shit together.

Lil Dbag, glad to see you got the whip cream off your face. How did that cherry taste with the belly button lint on it? At least the lint wasn't from his ass. Ask Julie how that was. Ass crack and taint—smelling lint, now that's some nasty shit. Not something you want to smell during the holiday season. I hate your team, and I hope Gurley breaks his leg.

Betty Cocker, glad to see I got a win over you by beating you like a rented mule on a ride to the bottom of the Grand Canyon. Get used to it, and oh yeah, fuck you.

Gene Wilder, how are the Oompa-Loompas? I hear you beat them and made them shine your shoes until they were like mirrors. How about providing some chocolate-covered footballs, you cheap fucker? All that chocolate and no one to eat it. I hear Lee Gandy is trying to get an Oompa-Loompa from you to have a three-way in the basement with his other midget. WTF? Don't give him one. They are people too. Kind of creepy, but people nonetheless.

That's Yur Baby, looks like you didn't get two wins this week. I would say I feel bad for you, but that would be a lie.

Asshole Licker, You got two more wins, so I fear it is time to slap the dick smell off your breath and give you a beatdown. Stay away from the Grizz's house. I hear he is locking people in his shed and making them carve pumpkins and eat raw fish. He calls it sushi, but it is the goldfish out of his tank in the basement. There is something seriously wrong with that man.

Grizzlemcfucknuts, here we go again. What the hell were you thinking? You show up to work wearing your sweatpants up to your chin and pulled tight against your junk. We can tell that you are circumcised and your sack looks like a bear claw missing the thumb. Your bottom lip is pulled over your top lip, and you have one eye looking east and the other looking west. And you have a hat that is six different colors with a propeller on top. Also, it was reported that you were holding balloons that said different things like "Iron my shirt, bitch" or "I was told there would be cake." One of my favorites was "I see stupid people" and one that just said "Fuck you." I hear they called you into the office to talk to you about your wardrobe decisions and about shitting behind your booth on the turnpike. Apparently, they let you go, and to add insult to injury, your crack-whore called you a loser and left with Ramsey in his Honda. Now please tell us what the hell you were thinking. I can't believe Ramsey would do that to you right after you pulled him out of his autistic coma with your ball sack trick.

Until next time. This is the Commish wishing you all a bout with leprosy. Commish out.

Another week

Another week is over, and yes, I know, a new week has started, and I am late writing this, so suck my asshole and get off my back. Jeez, what do you want from me? I am only one man. My team last week sucked the shit out of a troll's asshole with no barbecue sauce on it. WTF is wrong with my team? I know I am scraping the bottom, but don't ever count the Commish out or he just may sneak up on you and squirrel you right in the butthole. I am rambling, so I will stop for now and write some off-color shit about the rest of you because I know you like it.

Ramsey, I hear you got all moved into the Griz household and you are loving it. Word has it that the Griz has you on a gold chain attached to a silver-spiked collar. You are also wearing an assless vinyl jumpsuit, complete with the mask and a red rubber ball in your mouth to keep your piehole shut so he doesn't have to hear you screaming at the TV when the Redskins are losing. He did cut eyeholes in the hood so you can watch the game. How very fucking Christian-like of him. He also said he does not like it when the Redskins lose and he has to clean up your tears running down your shiny vinyl jumpsuit. Maybe it's just me, but I really think you need to shave that hairy ass of yours if you are going to keep wearing those assless chaps. Glad to see you are happy.

Lil Dbag, it looks like you lost another close one and won a close one. You might have won both if you didn't still have whip cream and belly button lint in your left eye. I have been trying to tell you to stay away from the Griz. Have you seen what he is doing to Ramsey? Sad, so sad, and just, maybe, a little wrong.

Bettycocker, you dirty whore, stay off the waiver wire. Other people need players too. I really thought your team would be doing better. I am glad they are not. Looks like you may need to Join Ramsey with some assless chaps at the Griz household. Yes, I will ask him to cut some eyeholes for you too. How else will you be able to shave Ramsey's hairy ass? It's pretty bad, so you may want to wax it. Do me a favor. If you use the wax and let a little drizzle onto his nut sack so when you pull the strip off, we can hear him try to scream through his red rubber ball gag and watch a tear run down his shiny black vinyl mask and drip onto the floor next to his goldfish and Pepsi can that he can't drink because his mouth is full.

Gen Fucking Wilder, you did it anyway. You gave Gandy an Oompa-Loompa, and now he is dead. Turns out Gandy liked tossing midgets so much that he started tossing Oompa-Loompas too. Guess he didn't realize that big old fivehead of theirs was so soft and there is no bone in there, and when he hit the curb headfirst, it killed him. Gandy took out an ad in the paper on the front page claiming he is the world's greatest midget thrower and is changing his name to "Gary Foster World's Greatest Midget Tosser." If you want to see him in action, get tickets to the next rodeo in Hill City, Kansas. I heard there will also be a horse-fucking exhibit at this particular rodeo.

Thatsurbabyshit, have you seen what your sons are doing? If I were you, I would be pissed with the Griz but maybe you want to join them at the Griz household. After all, he is the funny one.

Asshole Licker, how did the pumpkin carving go? Glad to see you made it through alive after eating all those goldfish. Ramsey wanted me to ask you to get off his back. Literally, get off his back because you are too heavy to be riding him around like a horse. He especially didn't like you riding him bareback with nothing on but spurs. He said he didn't mind the bareback so much because the sound your bare ass made sliding across the shiny black vinyl made it sound like you were farting and that makes him laugh. The bad part was when you dug your spurs into his ribs and yelled, "Getty up, bitch!" Daddy needs to get to the fish market." WTF is wrong with you, and what are you doing at the fish market?

Grizzlemcfuckstick, here we are again, and it seems like maybe you are having a bit of a party at your house. Not sure it's a party as much as it may be a cult you are starting. So I hear you did actually get a job at the hospital pulling people out of comas with your smelly nut sack trick. I hear it took some convincing, but the hospital board agreed to it after the demonstration showed it really works. They are dumbfounded that it works and want to do a study on you to see what kind of smell your body is producing that would snap people out of a coma. It has got to be just fucking rank. Whatever works, right? I hear you are, yourself, now in the hospital with a swollen left nut. Guess that 350-pound black guy didn't like waking up to you with your nut sack under his nose. Probably didn't help when he woke up and you were rubbing your left nut on his upper lip and saying, "You know you want it, bitch. Now take it all." I am guessing that is why he punched you in your nut. Lessons learned. Don't speak to the patient, and you need to tie their arms down so they can't grab your junk. Anyway, I hope your nut heals soon so you can get back home to your circus.

Until next time, when we find out if Ramsey gets a drink of Pepsi and the swelling goes down in Grizz's left nut.

Commish out.

Another week

Another week is over, and yes, I lost two more games, and my team is the worst it has ever been. I guess you will have that from time to time. They will all be fired next year, and I will be taking a shit on the doorstep at the Griz mansion. I know his crackwhore will try to eat it because I have been eating nothing but skittles for a week, and that is her favorite candy right after the famous chicklet she uses for a tooth, of course. I know she wants to taste the rainbow, but that is not the way to do it. She is dumb.

Ramsey, glad to see you got a drink of your Pepsi through a straw that was run through Betty Cocker's ass crack while you were drinking it. Sometimes I wonder what is wrong with you. You suck. The Cubs are gay, and you need a slap in the teeth. I hear you cried like a little bitch when BC waxed your asshole. I must confess. I asked her to drop a little on your sack because I wanted to hear you scream. At least you have a shiny new hairless butthole to show off when the Griz is parading you around the mall on a leash in public. I think it is nasty, and you should be wearing pants, but look on the bright side—now you get to wax her hairy asshole. You can be the hairless butthole twins. Just saying.

Lil Dbag, fuck you! I am glad Odell broke his leg. Did you see him crying on the field just like Ramsey when he got all his asshole hair removed. What a bitch. It ain't that bad.

BettycoCKer, thank you for waxing Ramsey. We were tired of looking at the little balls of shit wound up in his ass hair. It was just nasty and, of course, smelled like shit and Pepsi. I hear you are a little nervous that he is now going to wax your butthole so you can be twins. It will be all right, just take a squirrel to bite down on when he pulls off the wax strip. I am sure the Griz brought some of his furry little friends from the Unabomber country in Montana. Ask him sometime about the squirrels.

Gene Fucking Wilder, quit running up the scores, mother-fucker, or the Oompa-Loompa gets it. What do you feed them any-way? I hear all they eat is tree moss and pumpkin stems. That seems a little weird but may explain their pasty orange color. They seem a little creepy. What does their skin feel like? Have you ever fucked one? I hear Ricky Bumperhead from under the bridge in Butte wants to come live with you. He thinks he will blend in with them. I told him I didn't think so, but he is headed your way anyway. Be a dear and get some orange paint so he can blend please.

That's Yourbabyshit, I can't believe you are leaving me behind. I hear you were going to get your haircut. don't do it. Oh, I forgot to tell you that Brady said he needs shoes.

Asshole Licker, Ramsey says thanks for putting some pants on and getting off his back. What were you doing at the fish market? I hear you were buying nothing but fish heads for your retarded Chinese girlfriend. It's okay. They need loving, too, and just think that you can take her to the zoo where you like to go and feed the llamas and goats. I hear the Griz has a cage on wheels for you. There should be enough room for you and your Chinese pontard.

GrizzleMcfucknuts, how's the swelling in that left nut? I hope you learned your lesson about speaking when you are bringing peo-ple out of a coma with your smelly nut sack. Ramsey said to tell you thanks for the drink of Pepsi, but you didn't need to tie his arms behind his back and make him drink his Pepsi from a straw that ran the length of Betty Cocker's ass crack and into the Pepsi can. Secretly, I think he liked it. I haven't heard much out of your crackwhore. Is she still mad at you for mistaking her for a midget and tossing her across the yard? I hear you are taking up hang gliding, and your neighbors are pissed. Just doing it is one thing, but doing it naked is another. Your wife told me you drank an eight-pack of Mickey's Big Mouths beer and then put on one of those beer hats—the one that holds six bottles of beer. And they all had a straw that went to your mouth. The reason for the beer is a little disturbing. Apparently, you waited until you had to piss really badly and then you took off on your glider, swooping down really close to people you don't like, and before they could turn away fromlooking up and pointing at you, they realized you were pissing on them. Someone said they heard you saying, "Don't let me shit behind the church." Well, fuck you, and piss on everybody. What the hell is wrong with you? These are your friends and neighbors. Let me know how that works out for you.

That's it for this week. Tune in next week to see if Griz gets arrested for hang glider pissing.

Commish out.

Another week

I know I have not written, but it has been hectic, and sometimes I don't feel like it, so blow me. Anyway, I have to start with this: I won two games last week, and I love it. Of course, it will be short-lived, I am sure. This other one is a true story. Thatsurbaby told me the other day about our three-pound Yorkie named Tucker. She was lying in bed still half asleep when Tucker jumped on her face and stuck his little dick right in her mouth. Before she knew what was going on, he flipped around and dropped his nuts in her mouth, with his bunghole right on her nose. I was laughing about as hard as I had ever laughed, as she was saying, "That's not funny." His little peter was even a little wet. At that point, I was laughing so hard that no sound was coming out. I thought I would share that because it was so funny. Back to football. Well, back to writing stupid made-up shit about all of you.

Ramsey, we were all wondering if you had a good time waxing Betty Cocker's hairy butthole. However weird it seems, we want you two to know that we appreciate it. Although I am not sure which one is worse when you frame the bunghole with assless leather chaps: a hairy butt crack covering the hole or a hairless one that we can see your puckered O-ring. Anyway, thanks for doing that, and I hope you learned your lesson when you got arrested the other night. It turned out you were in the Walmart parking lot at 0300, right next to one of the cart returns, and you were snapping your carrot when a cop walked up and asked what you were doing. Being the honest homo that you are, you told him you were jacking while staring at the shopping carts. That is a sick fetish no one wants to hear about. Next time, don't park right beneath one of the lights, and for sure, don't sit on the hood of your car. It cast a shadow on the side of the building that made it look like King Kong was trying to pull off his cock really fast. The cops were laughing but arrested you for indecent exposure. Come on, man, get your shit together.

Lil Dbag, it looks like your team is falling apart, just like those fake shoes you paid $300 for that were actually from Korea, right off the street. Glad to see someone sucking as bad as me.

Gene Fucking Wilder, I thought I told you to quit running up the score? I guess you will have to have your sack speed bagged until it swells up like your dad's sack when he gets punched in the balls. I hear Ricky Bumperhead made it to your house and you made him cry because you wouldn't let him shine your canvas tennis shoes. That's fine, but leaving a full handprint, including the thumb on his giant forehead, wasn't the Christian thing to do. I do understand he is a bit if a biter, and you had to do it to get him off your kneecap before he bit it clean off. Next time, if you wet your finger and stick it in his ear, he will stop. He bit Griz one time just like that, and the Griz jammed a finger right up his ass, and he stopped biting and now hides from the Griz when he sees him. "Extreme times call for extreme measures" is what the Griz says. Bite me and I will violate your asshole.

That's Yourbabyshit, I would mess with you, but your team is biting a donkey's cock right now also, so that's a good thing. I need to make the playoffs.

Grizzle Mcfucknuts, well, here we go again, except this time, I am pretty sure Omeletting is not going to be an Olympic sport. You may be the first one to even say the word *Omeletting* and use it as a verb. I hear you got the idea from Retod and the Vag when you walked in on them. It seemed when you walked in, Retod was blowing a load in the Vag's ear. Being surprised, he just folded his ear over, and you thought it looked like an omelet. So you decided to make that a sport. Here's how it goes:

It would be a judged competition with points for the following:

- The size of load
- The fold staying and the length of time it stays
- Evenness (style points)

This is probably the sickest one you have come up with, and I am not sure how you got Asshole to agree to let you practice on him, but you two need to get out of the front yard before the cops show up and you are sharing a cell with Ramsey and his shopping cart. I tried to take the cart from Ramsey, but he said the cops said he could get one conjugal visit.

Until next time. The Commish says, "Never kick a fresh turd on a hot day."

Commish out.

Another week

Well, it's been a while, but then who gives a shit. I will write when I want to, and if I don't, you can lick my sack. My team has been doing a lot better. I just need enough wins to get in the playoffs, and then you fuckers are in trouble. The Commish has been putting up some good numbers, and if the matchups are right, you will all go down like Grizz's crackwhore on a donkey's cock on Christmas morning under Charlie Brown's fucked-up Christmas tree. Just saying.

Ramsey, I'm glad to see the injury bug bit you in the ass like it had some of the rest of us. Did you make any friends while you were in jail for jacking off in the Walmart parking lot? I heard some guy named Frank made you toss his salad with mayonnaise and horse radish sauce. I heard he actually put shredded lettuce in his ass crack for you to eat. Sorry about your bad luck, but I guess you won't be jacking off your junk in the parking lot anymore. Unless of course you like salad now and want a real date with Frank.

Li'l D'bag, I'm not sure how I like your team coming on like it did last week. You see how this week went? That's how it needs to stay. I need you to suck for the rest of the year. You stay focused on buying shoes and doing your nails, and leave the football to the men.

Gene Fucking Wilder, nice try this week, but it looks like I am going to beat you. That's karma for bitch-slapping Ricky Bumperhead's giant fivehead, including the thumbprint. Why would you slap a mentally disabled person anyway? I hear some of your resident Oompa-Loompas were down at the park terrorizing kids. Did you put them up to that? You know they frighten kids because they are orange and don't have any knees or elbows, and they have regular-sized heads and little bodies. It just looks weird and a little creepy even to me, and I am an adult. Not to mention they did not have pants on, and they have a regular-sized cock, so that also looks freaky on that little body. It looks like they are packing a big old mule dick dragging the ground. Anyway, you may want to get them on a leash.

Betty Cocker, it looks like you gave up. Let us know if you need to be tea bagged to get back in the game.

Asshole Licker, you had top players get hurt, and you were supposed to stop winning. You picked up scrubs and scored over two hundred points? What the hell. I think you might need a date with Ricky Bumperhead for a little pontard loving. Word has it that when Ricky gives you head, you know you have had head. That thing weighs sixty-three pounds and has a circumference of fifty-seven inches. That should take your mind off football, you sick fucker. You will lose both games next week even if I have to cheat. Good luck and be careful. He is a bit of a biter.

Grizzle McFucknuts, I would ask how you and Ass Licker's omelet making are coming along, but I don't care. I'm not sure cuming in someone's ear and folding it over to look like an omelet is going to catch on as an Olympic sport anyway. So please stop doing it to him in the front yard. Would you please get a grip on your crackwhore? I heard she was down in the gay district of town with a little cart, selling Jewish boy babies' foreskin to homos for bubblegum. Now I know this was not hurting anyone, but this was about as sick as you could get, I'm guessing. The fucked-up part was she had made eighty-three dollars and some change. I guess she was selling bottles of water also. I asked what the hell she was doing, and she said she was doing what you told her to do and that you gave her the seed money to get started in this business. I have to wonder where you get all these sick ideas and if I need to get you some help.

Have a fucked day.

Commish out.

Family League 2018

Week 1

Welcome back to the house of clowns for another beatdown like you are used to. I am going to try and write each week something sick and twisted because all you people like that, except for Thatsurbaby. She thinks the Grizzle McFucknuts is the funny one. She doesn't know any better. Poor little pontard doesn't know funny when it smacks her in the face with its big old cock.

Asshole, as your name states, you are an asshole, and you need to be spanked like you are one of Adrian Peterson's kids who broke a window and told his mom to fuck off and eat a dick.

Me: Look out, assholes, here I come for the top spot.

Grizzle McFucknuts, I never know what you are doing. Are you in Alaska shitting behind an igloo or in a bucket? Or are you in Montana doing some chiclet-toothed whore? You are like a wandering shit-anywhere-fuck-anything gypsy. You just need a Volkswagen van with a shit emoji painted on the front. I hear you moved out of Lincoln, and I bet the squirrels are sad. The squirrel ring leader told me in a press conference that they would get by, but they were worried the new owners wouldn't let the squirrels fuck them in the face like you did. Did you even consider taking the squirrels with you? I know you had a bond or, should I say, seal (your lips to their dick). Anyway, give it some thought, as they said they were willing to relocate to the lake just to be near your face. They also told me to tell you they didn't like it when you grabbed their ears and told them to go home because they were drunk. They said they didn't even drink. I think maybe you were the drunk one.

Ramsey, I see you are bringing up the rear in your division. Your mom told me it was because you talked so much about ass fucking that you deserved to be on the bottom getting ass fucked, and then she made that bend-you-over-hump-your-ass motion while whipping that ass. It was almost as funny, as the (with every heart beat motion in the Whitney song) only lane would get that one, but it was fucking funny. You will just have to take my word for it.

That's your baby, look at you leading the way. Too bad I waxed that ass last week, and let me tell you, it felt good, and I want some more. So bend over because I like it when you call me Big Papa. I know you won't read this because Doug didn't write it, so you won't think it's funny.

Steelhisvirginity, look at you go. I think maybe some beginner's luck because I know you can't see that well with the sack of a billy goat in your eyes.

Lil Dbag, way to stink it up this year. Maybe if you spent a little more time on football and a little less time shopping for shoes with your sister you might be doing better. Either way, you are a homo.

Lilmama, what can I say? Do you even have a team, and if you do, do they know their way to the stadium? Get your shit together and get on the waiver wire.

That's it this week.

Fuck you.

Commish out.

Another week

Well, another week is in the books, and I took three losses and even gave little mama her first win. Talk about a kick in the nuts. You all can suck on my ball hair. That's the long, stringy, and thin stuff hanging off the bottom that when I sit down is pressed up against my taint. Yes, that is the ball hair I am talking about you kissing.

Asshole, you know I hate you for winning so much, but you know it will not last. Just like last year, it will all come crashing down on your giant gourd of a head. Grizz says you need to shave your back hair because he keeps getting his hangnails caught in it.

Commish, what can I say? I had a shitty week, and believe me, I hated it. I hope to come back this week and punt all your balls to Cleveland with all the other losers.

Ramsey, fuck you and the whore you rode in on. You are supposed to be losing to me just like you usually do. Your mom called me and told me she saw you on the outdoor cameras humping my garden gnomes. Knock that shit off. What have they ever done to you? No matter what they taught you in school, humping garden gnomes will not turn them into leprechauns that have to grant you three wishes. That's just dumb. Put your pecker back in your pants and jack off to Walmart shopping carts like you usually do.

Grizzle McFucknuts, so what's up with the squirrels? Did you go get them so they can begin fuck starting your face again? I know they will be happy about that. Just remember not to grab their ears. They hate that for some reason but said they wouldn't mind a finger in the asshole if you don't mind. What's with your shitty record in the league? If you want one of the rings, you need to win games. Maybe you need to start praying while you are shitting in your new place at the lake. I heard your new lake neighbors are not exactly happy with your shitting habits. I will give them a call to see just what the fuck you are up to.

Thatbabybutt, I don't even know why I write about you in here since you don't read it. Or do you read it and don't want to admit that it's funny? Let's see if you are reading this. Fuck you in the asshole 'cause I know you like it. By the way, I can't stand it that you have a better record than me. I may need to change some of your players out when I play you. We will see if you are up to it or if your ass is too sore.

Steelhisvirginity, well, I do not like the way this is going. I am managing your team and doing better than I am with my own team. Guess that has to stop now that you are done with your STD medicine. I may have to have Brady kick you in the balls with one of his $400 tennis shoes.

Lil Dbag, fuck you! Stay off the waiver wire. Every time I go to get someone, your dirty little fingers have already been there. Put your dirty little fingers back in your ass where they belong. Your team sucks just like you. What a loser.

Lilmama, well, here is a giant fuck-you for beating me to get your first win. You really need to get your team together because they are sucking rhino cock right now, and that is a reflection of you. Pick it up, sister. You're making the family look bad.

That's it. Until next time. Let's see if Grizzle Mcfucknuts can beat the world record for shooting lint from his ass for distance.

Commish out.

Another week

Another week is in the books, and I know I did not write last week, so blow me. It was a good week for the Commish—three wins and a beatdown on Ass-licking-hole, so that was a bonus.

Asshole, looks like you took an ass beating like Tina Turner did from Ike Turner when she didn't do the dishes right after supper. How did you like losing two games this week? I loved it.

Ramsey, look at you go, dickhead. You lost half your team and still rocked it this week. I liked it better when your team was sucking. Let's go back to your team sucking, just like when you were sucking the balls of that clown who worked at McDonald's. I think his name was Ronald. I know you know his name because you were always humming it when you were slobbering on his cock. Don't forget to vote (inside joke). Your mom told me to tell you to quit trying to fuck Donkey in the ass because he doesn't like it.

Grizzle McFucknuts, so how was your week, squirrel fucker? Let's see. It looks like you lost all three because you were playing the three teams that scored the most points for the week. I did get a call from the neighbors, and it appears you had managed to piss them off already. They told me they saw you down at the edge of the lake and couldn't quite make out what you were doing, so they strolled on down to the lake to greet their new neighbor. As they approached the water, they could not believe their eyes. You were in knee-deep water and squatted down so your ass was in the water, and you were reading the newspaper, facing the sun that was coming up over the Rocky Mountains. Of course, they were appalled that you were taking a shit right there in the water and asked you what you thought you were doing. You replied, "Reading the paper and watching the sun come up. Oh yeah, and I am taking a shit, so if you don't mind, I would like a little privacy." What the hell is wrong with you? Their kids swim in the lake. And why was a squirrel sitting on your naked lap looking at the paper as though he was reading it with you? And why were you shitting in the lake? Why won't you use a toilet? What the hell is wrong with you?

That's your baby, if a clown fucked you in the ass and didn't give you a reach around, do you still think Doug is funnier than me? Who be touching my monkey balls? I'm wet.

Steelhisassvirginity, looks like I am doing well with your team. You suck. Get off my daughter. She's pregnant. Brady wants to fuck your brother. Have you ever had Cheetos dust on your balls?

Lil Dbag, I know you never read this, so fuck you in the mouth with a mosquito dick and his entire foreskin.

Lilmama, your team is so bad you need to hit the waiver wire or the bottle.

That is all. Please stay out of jail and off Gene Wilder's nipples. Commish out.

Another week

Another week is underway, and I know I have been gone for a few weeks, but I did not think I was gone long enough for the Griz to invent a new Olympic sport.

He called it Hula bowling, and I would think that it would only be played at a nuthouse, but who knew.

I will try to explain the rules to you as they were explained to me and then demonstrated to us in a live demo.

The first rule is you have to be at least fifty years old or you will never knock down the pins. You will know why as I explain the rules in greater detail.

You have to be a male of at least fifty years (the older the better). You need a Hula hoop (one from Walmart will work), or you can buy an expensive one or a plain one and bedazzle it if you like. The choice is up to you.

You need to be naked.

You need a set of bowling pins (six pins are used for this sport).

Draw a line eighteen inches in front of the pins. You can't pass this line.

Grab your nuts in one hand. Now you start up the hoop around your waist and get a rhythm going and let your nuts go and make sure they get in a nice rhythm with the hoop. When you are ready, you thrust your hips out at the right time to see how many pins you can knock down.

The rest of the rules are like bowling. Sounds easy, right?

Well, the demo was hilarious and probably did not go as planned. Captain Grizzlenuts, aka "King Hula Baller," in the Hula bowling world gave us a live demo.

We were in the backyard for this presentation, having a family barbecue, when Grizz asked us if we wanted to see something cool. It was a sport he invented.

Being a supportive family, we said, "Sure, why not. Anything is better than having to retrieve him from the back of the church with doggie baggies to clean up his shit."

Well, King Baller got naked, bent over at the waist, and grabbed his hoop (wish that would have happened in reverse order).

He cupped his balls in one hand and spun the hoop around his waist with the other.

As he gained momentum, he let his balls fly at just the right moment and knocked down all the pins for a strike, but the velocity was so great he couldn't rein the twins back in, and after they knocked down the pins, they hit Brady and knocked him clean out of the kiddie pool and the fruit loops right out of his mouth. They went on to knock over three chairs, pulled the umbrella right out of the ground, slammed the lid closed on the barbecue grill, and took a four-inch patch of fur off the neighbor's cat before reaching their final destination next to the screen door on the back porch.

I am not sure, but it looked painful. Not sure this will catch on, but what can you expect from someone that will shit outside behind the church with a one-toothed wanderer. Good luck on your patent and your demo for the Olympic committee.

Ramsey, I know how bad you want to take up Hula bowling, but there is no way you are old enough yet. You will understand why when you reach fifty.

That's it for this week. Until next time. Try not to step on your sack and don't let the cat play with your balls.

Commish out.

That's it for this family league saga. I hope you enjoyed it. Keep reading for the pick'em league write-up.

PICK'EM FOOTBALL

List of characters

Grizzlenuts, you met this big burley guy in section 1. He is still the same outside-shitting, crackwhore-fucking, squirrel-licking, and Olympic-sport inventor he was in section 1. I will tell you that he did jump in the air, do a 360, pull down his sweatpants (no underwear), separate his ass cheeks while in the air, and shoot lint from his pucker onto his wife's cheek. I'm pretty sure she did not like that. That takes talent and a type of sickness I am not sure I can relate to.

Retod (Todd), that's funny because he is from Boston area, so I call him Retodded. If you don't get it, that's okay because you are probably retarded. He is about sixty years old with thinning blond hair. He is usually a happy guy and loves to play tennis, which is a gay sport. I am not saying he is gay, but I am pretty sure his boyfriend is.

The Vag is a short, skinny guy who is very funny. He is a joy to be around and says he owns a unicorn, but I doubt that. I'm pretty sure he likes to play tennis as well.

Perks My Little Ponies is a Billy Ray Cyrus—looking fucker. I am sure he was sporting a trendy mullet in the eighties. He is a nice guy unless he is drunk; then I am guessing he is probably a big dickhead. He is a sports nut who used to pitch professionally. He is an all-around nice guy, you know, for a gay left-handed cross-dresser.

31

Elknuts—we met him in section 1, but I can assure you he is even a bigger pole-smoking douchebag in section 2. He still looks like Homer Simpson with a big old water head and shoes that makes him look like he is wearing clown shoes. Don't tell him that because he is very sensitive and may cry himself to sleep on his huge pillow.

Looking for 5 dicks is a weight lifter, welder, and complete asshole. He may be getting mellow in his old age, but I doubt it. He was one of the very few who had the balls to give the commissioner shit. It wasn't really funny, but at least he tried. Most of these dicks did not have the balls to give the commissioner shit.

Grape Ape is a blond and fat ex-marine who looks a lot like a bag of doughnuts that has been beaten with a rawhide mallet. He is pretty good at picking the games but not as good as he thinks he is. Apparently, he likes to write poetry in his spare time. I hope I don't see him hanging out with Retod and the Vag anytime soon. I don't think he is a pole smoker, but you never know. He was a marine.

Ganderkonz is kind of a gangly sloth-like creature. He is an easygoing guy just eking his way through life. He gets a lot of shit from the Commish but takes it all in stride because he knows it's just for fun and to make people laugh. He has a personal fetish with fucking midgets. I'm not sure why he likes that, but it is his dick, so it's his call. He also likes to toss them for distance and actually hit Griz up to try and make it an Olympic sport.

Jokie is one of the nicest, clean-cut, church-going, hokie fan, and family-loving guy you will ever meet. He looks like Denny Hamlin, the NASCAR driver. He is that guy who everyone likes. Just don't tell his family he laughs at what the Commish writes and craves the write-up each and every week. He is, deep down, just as sick as the Commish. He also cross-dresses and runs a gay strip club. I bet his pastor doesn't know that little nugget of information, or maybe he does since I saw him come out of the club one time at two o'clock in the morning. I figured he was just in there witnessing and spreading God's message. I guess he could have been in there getting his face glazed like a doughnut. Don't ask; don't tell, "Right, Preacher?"

Sack Attack used to be a lifeguard, so we know that he, at a minimum, is bisexual. He is not very tall, and he is kind of dumpy. I'm pretty sure he is into she-males and pegging. I heard he sent Retod and the Vag a private message, asking them if they were interested in giving him bukakke. They said yes, and last I heard, they were setting up a date for the festivities. I heard they even hired a band for this party. The Commish will not be attending such a shindig.

Gash changed her name from Zombie Girl to Gash. It's pretty close to right on. She is one of the few women in the league and the only one to actually give the Commish any shit. She is not the best at it but not too bad either. She was no match for the Commish, but at least she tried. The Gash actually did pretty well in the league and finished near the top or on top the years she played.

Pick'em 2017

Next week, the Thursday games will be put back in the lineup. The majority wants it, so that's what is going to happen. I know some of you don't like that but too fucking bad. Get used to it and get your picks in early.

Listen up, dickheads, and get your fingers out of your mud whistles. If you have paid, thank you, and if you haven't, then you need to put a cheek in each hand and carry your ass to the ATM and get the money to me so I can run the numbers to see what the payouts will be.

Looks like Retod and the Vag will be joining us again this year. You will be ridiculed as much as my imagination can handle. So saddle up your unicorn and put on your pink stirrups and assless chaps. This should be fun for the rest of us.

Quit laughing, Perks My Little Ponies! I will be riding you bareback also. You may want to start doing deep knee bends over a fire hydrant to get loosened up. That way it will not hurt so much when Elknuts fists you every Sunday. I know you like it, but last year, you didn't loosen up or lube up, and you whined all season about how your ass burned.

I heard that 5 Dicks got caught blowing Tom Brady without his permission. Tom wasn't too mad. He doesn't mind cheating on the football field but doesn't like to cheat on his wife. Settle down, Ray. Tom is not a Greek god. He and Bill need to quit cheating because they suck at it. They are always getting caught.

Don't worry, Grizzlenuts, I wouldn't leave you out. I heard you were going to barber school 'cause you wanted to open your own shop, trimming and frosting ball hair. What the hell is wrong with you? You need to pay a little bit more attention to your picks instead of all that taint hair you will be dying different colors. I heard Retod and the Vag already have appointments set up for a trim and some pink ball-hair dye.

Just a little taste of what you will be reading this year if you stay tuned.

PS. Buckle up for safety, Gandy, because you will be featured next week after the first week is on the books.

Commish out.

Week 1

Well, week 1 is in the books, and you don't have to tell me I suck. I just cannot seem to get any higher than the middle of the pack. Fuck, I hate that. Oh well, there are a bunch of you below me, so that makes me feel better.

Retod and the Vag, looks like you two are near the top of the pile, but aren't you usually bent over the pile, if you know what I mean? I believe I will have to remove some of your points because just like the Patriots, I know you cheated. Turns out I am friends with one of the ESPN reporters, and she told me she overheard a conversation between you two about some point-shaving and inside information. The story goes like this: You two were seen in the locker room of the Patriots because Tom Brady hired you guys to be what they call in the porn industry fluffers. Although you offered to do that part for free, what you really wanted was the info on the games that were going to be thrown, like the Pats against the Chiefs. I will have to take fifty points from each of you to show you that cheating is only allowed by the commissioner. Shame on you two.

We have some new comers, like Vanilla Gorilla, who will now be known as Grape Ape. You will be ridiculed relentlessly in here, so keep an eye out for reports on Grape Ape. I saw him a few minutes ago, and he was deep throating a monkey pickle (banana for you, fucktards). I will admit his eyes were watering, and he was gagging, so he is not a pro just yet, but give him time. Fag.

Grizzlenuts, you also sucked the shit out of a dead donkey's asshole this week. I guess you did not have time to concentrate since you and your chicklet-toothed crackwhore got jobs as toll booth attendants on the Jersey turnpike. To be honest, you are the only one that got the job. They just let her stand in the one that people throw their change in. Poor thing thinks she is actually counting the money they throw in there. So dumb! Oh yeah, I went by there the other day, and the thin candy coating is wearing off her chicklet tooth and is starting to look like a piece of plumber's putty. Be a dear and get her a fresh chicklet will you, please. It looks nasty. Not that she does not look nasty enough weighing in at sixty-seven pounds and is five feet, nine inches tall. Anyway, don't forget there is a Thursday game this week. Try to make some reasonable picks this week.

There are some ladies in the league, so please watch your mouth and keep the cussing to a minimum. Just joking. There are no ladies in the league. There are some bitches who think they know football though. Welcome aboard, and if you get offended easily, then don't read any of these commissioner messages.

Perks my little ponies, WTF! You suck. I guess you have been spending too much time in your wiener mobile dressed up like a clown doing little kids' birthday parties. Take the rubber dick off your nose and pay attention. By the way, you know it is supposed to be a red rubber ball and not a dick on the end of your nose, don't you?

I still need money from one person. You know who you are, you Tom-Brady-ball-licking transvestite.

Mr. and Mrs. Cooper, get a room. Not one to fuck in, but one to make a little sense out of your picks. I expect more out of this supercouple—keeping up with the Coopers.

Lee fucking Gandy-Ganderkonz, I am thinking your leather football helmet is strapped a little tight. Your picks sucked. I am not sure why your mom called me, but she did. She told me you are still living in her basement, and she wants you out. Apparently, the other night, she got up to get a warm glass of milk and a shot of bourbon to help her sleep, and she heard some weird noises from the basement. She went down to check on you, and you were roasting an opossum over an open fire with a naked midget on your back. She said you were wearing a cowboy costume like Woody from *Toy Story*. What the hell is wrong with you, and where did you get a naked midget? Anyway, she wants you out.

That's it for this week. Until next week. Save a snatch and ride a bunghole for a change.

Commish out.

Another week

Well, week 2 is in the books, and I did a little better but hope to improve next week. I really must find a way to cheat.

Retod and the Vag, looks like your point-shaving scheme didn't pay off. So I guess you blew Tom Brady for nothing. Not that I am surprised, due to all the cheating he and Bill do every year. You two were so far apart on the chart this week that we almost thought you weren't a couple. Don't get all pissy. We know you two are together for life. Life partners, turd burglars, butt pirates, or whatever the politically correct term is. Just remember to keep it behind closed doors because we don't want to see you on your knees. You see what happened to Kaepernick for getting on his knees. Douchebag.

Grape Ape, looks like you need to pull that monkey pickle out of your ass and pay attention. I actually gained a few points on you this week.

Grizzlenuts, what the fuck were you thinking? Looks like you had your head in your ass this week, spending too much time with that crackwhore of yours. I heard your new job on the turnpike is going well except for your bitch getting hit twice after she started chasing some of the cars out of the booth like a dog. I honestly don't know what you see in her. Anyway, when you go to see her in the hospital, please take a picture of that tire mark on the side of her face.

We need a good laugh. I can't believe she has a tire tread mark all the way across her right cheek. Thank you for getting her a new chicklet to put in. The old one was looking just plain nasty.

Perks my little ponies, WTF! Have you gotten the cock off your face yet? Please do. It's very disturbing.

Lee fucking Gandy-Ganderkonz, I see you are up to your old tricks. Have you talked to your mom since she saw you with that naked midget? She was pretty disturbed by the mental picture of a naked midget on your back with his little short legs straining to wrap around your chest and his ball sack draped down your spine. She said it was an image she would never unsee. Anyway, I was thinking you should probably get your own place if you are going to be doing little people in the basement. What the hell is wrong with you?

JE Hokie, now known as "Jokie Hokie," welcome aboard. Just make sure you don't bring that Hokie bullshit attitude with you. What the fuck is a Hokie anyway? You will lose here, just like the Hokies.

Zackattack, aka "ASScrackLicker," you suck ass and are getting lucky. You will go down, and I don't mean on a goat either, so don't get excited. Besides, that Gandy ate the goat you blew last year. He cooked it over an open flame while wearing ski boots, a mask, and a snorkel. So you will have to find a new girlfriend.

Crushthewebster, your new name is "I Wanna Be like Mike," not doing too well in the pool. Maybe you should try your hand at Hula bowling or, should I say, try your balls.

Intercoursey, what the hell? This is not golf. We are not looking for the lowest score. You may want to get rid of the Lifetime channel and get ESPN and watch it. Wow!

That's it until next week, and remember to never lick taint on the first date.

Commish out.

Another week

Well, here we are with week 3 in the books. It was a pretty shitty performance by most everybody. I guess I should have done random picks last week. I probably wouldn't have done much worse. I am still hanging at that thirteenth spot, just waiting to pounce and fuck the shit out of all of you any way I can, just like my three-pound dog Tucker. He will fuck anything, anywhere, and anytime. I have actually seen him try to fuck a pig, a chicken, my wife's face, and of course, Grizz's crackwhore, which he actually accomplished.

Retod and the Vag, I guess we know who is the man in the relationship. It looks like Retod is on top, just like the football pool. Vag, maybe you should stick to doing Retod's toenails while he is watching the game. I saw you two at the Dairy Queen (how fitting) sharing a sundae, holding hands, touching feet, and smiling at each other. You know, in general, just gaying up the day. Get a room, and for fuck's sake, watch some football instead of reruns of the *Brady Bunch* because you know the dad is gay.

The Great Grape Ape, I see you won this week. Maybe you can put that money to good use, like for bail. Try to remember no means no.

JE Jokie, I see you are still riding the pine below me right where you like to be. I was thinking maybe you and TDUB could get a job putting glitter on strippers in the strip club. That would at least get you off sniffers' row at the club. Last time, you passed out facedown on the stage with a row of quarters in your hand. You're lucky those girls didn't beat your ass for throwing quarters at them and telling them you were going to make it rain and threw a handful of quarters at them. That's more like acid rain and not what they are looking for. And the answer is no, you cannot borrow money out of the football pool fund to pay for lap dances from big titty Betty. She is just nasty anyway. You would get lost in her ass crack. Luckily, when your wife came in looking for you, you had slid under the chairs next to the stage where she couldn't see you. No telling what's on that floor right next to the stage on sniffers' row. Get it together, man. You are better than that.

Zombiegirl aka "Gash," you must be one of those *Walking Dead*. Well, no one in here is dead, so make sure you are paying attention or we will have to send Grape Ape to club you like a baby seal. Of course, then we could make some coats or slippers. That would be nice. Anyway, welcome aboard and watch your back 'cause there are some Hokie fans in here. What the hell is a Hokie?

Cornhole Radical, I hold you personally responsible for Colin Kaeperfucks escapades. You are going to ruin football with that bullshit. Don't make me come over there and kneel on your chest. Your picks suck a fat baby's ass, by the way.

Lee fucking Gandy, here we are, three weeks deep, and you are still fucking midgets in your mom's basement. I think it may help if you venture out a little bit and lay off the little people. Remember how you used to put on your leather helmet, green army coat, snorkel and mask, ski boots, and a black leather thong? You had that life-size cutout of Neil Diamond that you sat in the seat next to you on the bus to talk to. Let's not forget the cherry-flavored spray you sprayed the windows with so when you licked them with that big, thick tongue, it tasted good. Good times. This time, stay off the courthouse steps yelling that you are going to bomb the place if they don't bring back *Gilligan's Island*. Anyway, just a thought to give your mom a break from listening to you stretch out the bungholes of the midgets in the basement.

Grizzlenuts, let's see what you have been up to this week. I hear you are about to lose your job at the toll booth. I am not sure why, but I did hear you got caught taking a shit behind your booth. Guess you didn't realize there are cars coming from the other direction also, and they saw your big old hairy asshole dropping a deuce onto the sidewalk. What the hell is wrong with you? One little old lady reported that at first glance, she thought a bull got out of the pasture when she saw the size of that wrinkly, stretched-out ball sack just grazing the ground. You need to knock that shit off and start using a bathroom. What is it with you and shitting outside? You need to pay attention to the football pool. You are losing your ass.

Let's not forget Perksmylittleponies. I see you finally got the cock off your face, but it left an imprint like those guys that wear masks for sleep apnea. I thought I caught a hint of a ball mark also, but I could be wrong. I hear you gave up the clown gig and were thinking about joining Grizzlenuts on the turnpike. Just be careful, and for fuck's sake, don't fuck his crackwhore. He is sensitive about that. Keep us posted if you end up on the turnpike. Just an FYI, they have a bathroom to shit in, so don't believe Griz when he says they don't.

Until next time. Never lick a cheerleader's asshole after a high-scoring football game. It tastes nasty and has no nutritional value.

Commish out.

Another week

I must say that the way I have been picking, I should maybe take up Hula bowling instead of picking winners in the NFL. At least I am not as big of a loser as these turd-licking assholes taking a knee. We need to keep politics out of sports. If you want to protest something, then do it on your own time. I am not condoning disrespecting this country at any time. If you want to burn a flag or kneel on it, all I got to say is don't let me catch you because I will stab you in the neck. If you don't like it here, then get the fuck out, but don't disrespect the flag or the men and women who died protecting your sorry fucking pansy asses. You play a game for a living and get paid way too much to do that. If I were king, I would put a sniper in each stadium and dare your punk ass to take a knee. To those taking a knee, I say, "Fuck you and kiss the inner pucker ring of my bunghole, you piece of bug-infested rotting camel foreskin." Rant over for now, but I can't promise anything. Can you tell I am more than a little pissed about these fucks?

Retod and the Vag—when last we left them, they were at the Dairy Queen gaying up the day. Word has it that you were on your way over to the Griz household for a slumber party. Griz is a pretty nice guy but not sure how he is going to react to you two over there in your tube tops and spandex. I know you wanted to take a Hula bowling lesson but not sure if the Griz wants you at his house with your nuts out swinging at his bowling pins. He said thinking about letting you two do that makes it seem gay. Maybe you could try the sheeting game he came up with. I'm sure he won't mind you stepping on his crackwhore's gut, especially since she called him a loser for losing his job on the turnpike. Anyway, good luck at the Griz place. Don't get him drunk. He gets violent, and you may end up tossing his salad. Watch out for the lint balls. They smell like ball sweat and shit.

The Great Grape Ape is now in first place, but you know how it is when you are on top. They want to bring you down. Well, here goes. I did find the diary you are writing. I can say I am not surprised that it is written in purple crayon and everything is in caps. I can't tell if you wrote this with one of your feet or one of your paws, but I will try to translate what I can only assume is a poem. I hope this is not real, but to each his own. The poem goes like this:

> I fucked a dead whore on the side of the road
> I knew right away that she was dead
> The skin on her belly was rotten
> She had nary a hair on her head
> And when my horrible deed was done
> I realized my terrible sin
> So I put my lips to her asshole and sucked out the
>   wad I shot in.

Now I don't know about the rest of you, but I have no idea where this sick shit comes from. That's just nasty, Grape Ape. I later found out you stole this from the Griz.

Je Hokie, I hope the wife didn't catch you at the strip club you had been living at. Give it up and go home. You may need to join ASA (alcoholic strippers anonymous). Just a thought.

Gash, I still hate you because you are beating me. I find it hard to believe a retired stripper, now bartender is kicking my ass in football picks. Is there a little dyke in you also? Not judging, just wondering and pissed because I am sucking, but at least it's not a cock I am sucking. We will leave that to Retod and the Vag.

Lee Fucking Gandy, how was your bus ride? The people who clean the buses are pissed. They are having a hell of a time getting the flavoring off the window you sprayed on there. They are not sure if it's the flavoring or the crusty white stuff from the corners of your mouth mixed with lung butter. Either way, they are not happy about it. I can tell you that I am not happy about bailing you out of Jail. How many times have I told you that you have to wear pants when you ride the bus? They are not buying the fact that you identify as a pair of pants, therefore you are wearing pants. That only works if you are a man and identify as a woman so you can use the women's toilet. I have explained this to you. Loosen your chin strap on that leather helmet and pay attention.

Grizzlemcfucknuts—not much to report this week on the Grizz. Just beware, Griz, the traveling homos Retod and Vag are headed your way for some Hula bowling or sheeting. Be nice. They are harmless. I wouldn't bend over naked in front of them, but they are harmless. Gandy is on the bus, also headed to your house. He said he has an idea for yet another Olympic sport. He got the idea when he got tired of that naked midget's sack rubbing a bare spot on his spine and tossed him across the room. So the idea is naked-midget tossing for distance. Kind of like shot-putting, but I wouldn't throw them from your cheek like you do a shot put. Their balls and ass stink bad because they cannot reach them with their short little arms. Anyway, you grab them by the ankles and swing until you reach max RPMs and then let go, thrusting them down the field as far as you can. After listening to his pitch on midget tossing, I thought, *Hey, what about midget bowling?* Anyway, he is on his way over in his ski boots and snorkel. Don't let him get in the kiddy pool. I promise he will piss in it.

That's it for this week. Never, and I mean never, let a bobcat jerk you off.

Commish out.

Another week

I know I am still sucking, so you don't have to tell me. I am more worried about getting these fucks to show some respect. Maybe we need to take a page out of the book of the coach for Virginia Tech basketball and make them stand in front of a wounded veteran and see if the piece of shit takes a knee then. Anyway, I think they should all be gang-raped and then fired. Just my opinion, but I like my opinion and don't give a fuck if someone doesn't agree.

Grape Ape, the *Great* is gone because you sunk so low this week. Must be the bad publicity from that psychotic poem you wrote and I shared. I found another one that I thought I would share with the crowd to show them how dismantled your thought process is. Here goes.

> There once was a beautiful yellow bird
> Singing so shrill
> Who landed upon my windowsill
> I hate birds, and I don't know why
> I guess because, for some reason, they make me cry
> So I lured him in with a piece of bread
> And then I crushed his fucking head

Now I don't know about the rest of you, but I am pretty sure that is the mind of one sick gorilla. Get your shit together and your anger under control. Come on, man!

Retod and the Vag, it looks like you ended up at the Griz household. How are you liking that? I hear he has you tied up and lying in his kiddie pool, drinking fuzzy navels and cleaning his feet.

JE Jokie, nice to see you out of the strip club. I bet your wife was glad you were out of that shithole but probably disappointed when you ended up in a gay bar called Nipples and Dicks. Josh, go home before you get squirreled in the ass at that gay bar. You won't like it.

Gash, I still hate you because you are beating me, and based on your comments, I don't know whether to knock the dick or pussy off your breath. I hate losing, especially to a rookie in this league. Anyway, fuck you and your winning.

Perksmylittlepony, where the fuck have you been? I hear you have been running around the country looking for yourself. I didn't want to believe it when I heard you were hanging out with Kaitlin Jenner. I guess we can ask you now. Has it had the operation yet or does it still have one meat and two veg? I understand. Don't kiss and tell, but this is different. You know that's gross, right? Anyway, don't be showing up to any football parties with her or you may get your ass kicked. I guess you don't mind if she takes a knee during the game, right?

Lee fucking Gandy, glad to see you are wearing pants again. I know the people on the city bus are happy not to have to look at your tick-infested ball sack. It just didn't look right watching you pick the ticks off your sack. Especially the ticks that had dug in really good and attached to your balls. When you pulled on them, it stretched your sack out, and when they let go, your balls would slap that cold blue fiberglass seat. One little old lady said she thought someone was slapping a dolphin. Okay, she might be a little crazy, but no one wants to see a grown man naked on the bus wearing a tube top, ski boots, a diving mask, and a snorkel, wearing no pants and picking ticks off his nuts. Come on, man, get it together.

Grizzlemcfucknuts, I hear you have Retod and the Vag under control at your house, getting drunk while washing your feet. WTF. You have them in your kiddie pool. Why do you have a kiddie pool? Oh yeah, that's right, to soak your swollen nuts in after a few games of Hula bowling. Gandy said you made him leave the kiddie pool because you were scared of ticks. You are too big to be scared of ticks. Are you sure it just wasn't the sight of him stretching out his scrotum to get the ticks off? He said you had him in a cage on wheels. What the fuck were you doing putting people in a cage? That doesn't sound right, but his mother wanted to thank you and see if you needed any money to keep him in there. She also wanted your address so she could send that naked midget to him. She said he kept trying to climb on her back naked, and he was messing up her hair and kept knocking off her glasses. Right now, she had his huge head super-glued to the siding on the garage until she got your address. I am beginning to think Gandy might be missing a few marbles. Anyway, glad to see you are having a good time, Lord knows you suck at the football thing.

Until next time. Never spit in your grandma's hair. She doesn't like it. It's just wrong, and it actually makes you an asshole.

Commish out.

Another week

I know I did not write last week. Consider it my bye week. Not that it matters since I can't pick the winners worth a shit. Don't laugh 'cause most of you suck as bad as I do. The only good part for me is writing shit about all you assholes. Let's see where I left off. I think Grape Ape was writing new poems, and the Grizz was caging people up. Let's see what happened.

Grape Ape, I did read another one of your poems, and this one referred to the football pool. I thought it was kind of funny, so here goes:

> I joined the football pool
> 'Cause I thought it would make me cool
>
> Turns out I cannot pick the winners, and I wish
>   I could
> Guess I will stick with what I know best, which is
>   punishing my morning wood
>
> Now from time to time, I have a good week
> But it goes to shit when I see porn because I have
>   to give that a peek
>
> Once I was actually in first
> But I blew that lead 'cause of my thirst
>
> Got drunk and kissed a toad
> Then swallowed a troll's nasty load
>
> I joined this league to try and win money
> 'Cause I'm not making any money trying to be
>   funny
>
> That's the end of this poem
> I need to go ass fuck a gnome

45

What the fuck is wrong with you, Grape Ape? You got some sick shit in your head.

Retod and the Vag, how is your time at the Grizz household? I hear he has you locked up in a cage eating nothing but skittles and drinking Pabst Blue Ribbon nasty-ass beer. All I can say is don't let him blindfold you or your ass will be sore for a week.

JE Jokie, WTF? I tell you to leave the gay bar and go home, so what do you do? You buy the fucking place, leave your wife, and shack up with a he/she called Kaitlin Jenner. The only thing worse would be if you decided to tea bag Hillary "Kunt" Clinton. I think it might be time for an intervention.

Gash, I see you are still whipping my ass. Are you sure you don't have a dick? I may have to change some of your picks this week. You can tell me. Who is really making your picks for you?

Perks Mylittle ponies, I don't know if you heard, but Jokie has been seen hanging out with your new bitch, Kaitlin. Rumor has it they moved in together. Now I know you probably want to kick his ass, but think about it before you react. Is Bruce really worth going to jail for? You have a wife and kids to think about, and I'm sure your boys don't want to know what you have been doing with Bruce. I'm sure it is nasty and illegal in some states, you sick motherfucker. Jokie says you weren't man enough for her anyway. He says he knocks the wind out of her by dick punching her lungs from the inside. Now I don't know if that's possible, but that is what he said. Again, that is just disturbing. Anyway, let me know if you need to talk or if you need the number for a good counselor. Maybe you could get in your wiener mobile and head down to the Griz cult.

Lee fucking Gandy, hope you got rid of the tick issue. I am still laughing about that lady who said that when your nuts hit the fiberglass bench seat on the bus, she thought someone was slapping a dolphin. You might want to stay away from the president. I heard you were following him around and yelling shit at him like "Build the wall, get a real haircut so you don't look like a Chiapet, cut taxes, pay off my mom's house, and give me a ride home, fucker." Luckily, he thinks you are harmless and just a little crazy. What the hell is wrong with you? You are going to get arrested, and then no more bus rides or fucking midgets in your mom's basement. Then what are you going to do?

Grizzlemcfucknuts, so I see you have been hanging around Gandy too long and have lost your mind. Your filthy crackwhore spilled the beans and told me your plans with all the people in the cages. You are taking them on the road like a circus and charging people to come by and stare at them and laugh. She showed me some of the signs that I will share with the football world:

> Grape Ape: Come see the blond-haired, dick-smacking poet who will write you a poem for $20.
>
> Retod and the Vag: Come see the homo couple eat skittles and shit rainbows that they will mold into art just for you for $20.
>
> Je Jokie: Come see what he learned at the strip bar, pole dancing at its best. You might want to wear earplugs because the sound his bare scrotum makes on that brass pole is very high pitched and has made three dogs go deaf. He gets into his work for $5 cover charge, and then slip him what you want if you like his dancing. For an extra $20, you can see him tea bag Kaitlin Jenner. Gross!
>
> Gash: Come see the only lesbian with a dick the size of a baby elephant's trunk for $20.
>
> Gandy: Come see the crazy fucker toss midgets for distance for $5.
>
> Captain Grizzlenuts: MC and owner of the fucked-up circus.

Please don't eat shit because it tastes like shit. That is just good advice.

Commish out.

Another week

Well, here we are again. Only this time, I have fallen farther down the list. I just can't seem to get the picks right unless they are for someone else. Even though I have fallen that far, it does not mean I will not be giving you all a bunch of shit anyway. We should start with a "Fuck you" and finish with an "in the ass."

Grape Ape, you motherfucker, you won again. The nice thing about that is that it was the fifty dollars Vinny gave me, so that means he can't win his money back. That and because he is gay and likes to ride Perk's Pony bareback. What a sick man. I heard you wrote another poem. Are you going to share it with us?

> Wasn't sure I wanted to play this game
> But I decided to do just the same
>
> I know I wanted to win lots of money
> Especially from Vinny, Perk's little honey
>
> Turns out I have won twice
> So I'm up fifty dollars from Vinny, and that
> makes it nice
>
> I plan on winning more
> Unless that cockblocker zombie girl wins, that
> fucking whore
>
> Not sure where she came from, but she needs to
> return
> Before someone slaps her hard enough that she
> ends up in an urn
>
> All you fuckers stay away from the money
> I need it so the wife will give me her pot of honey

That's it for this poem
Go home

Retod and the Vag, I'm glad to see you got away from the Grizz. That is a hard thing to do. It's like the Hotel California over there. Make sure you don't go to his cabin in Montana next to the Unabomber. He will have you eating squirrel nuts, drinking wild turkey, and reading Shakespeare out loud behind the church where he likes to take a shit. Don't ask me why because I do not know. I asked him one time, and he said he liked to shit there because he felt close to God, and the Shakespeare thing helped push shit through his colon, was what he said. Anyway, if you do go, do not be humping each other in public. They don't take to kindly to homos in Montana.

Jokie, so you sold your gay strip club and moved back home. I think you made a wise decision. I know you are going to miss all those boys dressing up like girls and stripping, but now you have your wife, who is a real girl, as far as I know, but that's your business. Someone told me you got into real estate, but flipping outhouses is not real estate. I think that is just the shit business. Call it what you want, but I wouldn't put a kitchen in one.

Gash, what do I have to do to get you to slow down? You don't just come into someone's house and take over the first year. All I got to say to you is "Fuck you."

Perks Mylittleponies, I see Josh moved back home, so you can have Kaitlin back, or you, too, can go home or do what you want. I see you must have been fucking a blind squirrel and got his nut because you finally got a win. I had your money, but I put it in Jokie's G-string, which he was wearing when he was dancing at Grizz's house on that brass pole. He really needs to oil up that sack so it doesn't make a squealing sound when he is sliding up and down that pole. It is a god-awful sound. Anyway, fuck you, and I hope you break your little toe. Not really, but that popped into my head.

Lee fucking Gandy, I see you are back at it, and your mom is scared to death that you are in some cult. I asked her why, and she said, "He has been in the basement for days with these orange things with green hair." Sometimes she would hear humming and screaming like someone is getting sacrificed. I calmed her down and told her they were Oompa-Loompas—just painted midgets—and you weren't killing anyone, and you were just dry fucking their asses, and that was why they were screaming. The humming was from when he would feed them chocolate bars and brush their hair. I told her she has nothing to be scared of, but she does have one sick motherfucker for a son.

And to finish, "Blow me."

Commish out.

Season 2018

We had a few people quit, but we picked up a few new people, so welcome aboard, losers. Please leave your feelings at the door because the odds of them getting hurt are relatively high. If you are easily offended, please come see me, and we will get you a kick in the balls or twat. Whatever applies to your personal situation. You will need to leave your liberal roots behind to be a part of The House of Asses. We don't play nice here. Please give me shit so I can give it back. I dare you.

The payouts will be the same this year, as noted below. The jackpot for picking every game right during the regular season starts at $510 and going up every week by $10. For you morons who can't read plain English, that means it does not count during the playoffs.

Good luck and fuck you in the ass until it hurts.

Commish out.

Week 1

What exactly is a cock waffle? Never heard that one. Last I heard, TDUBYA, you were making an omelet with Elkdawg's ear. You know how that goes. You blow a load on his ear and fold it over so it looks like an omelet. Then you sit on his ear to keep it warm. I know you told him it was good for his earache, but secretly, he does not have an earache. He just likes your little Keebler elf jizz in his ear. You two are sick, and I'm not sure I can let you stay in the league.

The new guy got it backward. What a maroon. He is right, though. If he had done it right, he would have kicked all our asses. You would think he would know better and follow directions, being in the nuclear business. We will have to keep an eye on him to make sure he doesn't hurt himself while he is texting and driving.

First week always sucks because it is just a crapshoot, but some of you really sucked a fat baby's ass, and you should be ashamed. Maybe next week you will pull your head out of the babysitter's ass and make better picks, but I doubt it.

Just so everyone knows, Zackattack and Naxsty still have not paid, so if you see them, please punch them in the neck and take their wallet. Remember, you two douchebags, you can't win if you haven't paid, so get me the money, or by week 3, you will be eliminated from the earth, or I will send you to Grizz's house to watch him Hula bowl. You may even be one of the pins he knocks down. If you don't remember what Hula bowling is, just give me a call, and I will explain it to you.

Retod and the Vag, you two still together? I heard you had a falling out over who gets top. Remember there is no such thing as a unicorn or anything that is "fun for the whole family."

Didyousaymuffins, you know, with a name like that, you are begging to get ass fucked and to be fucked with. Were you in the Girl Scouts or an all-boy band? Please tell me your wife named your team and you did not come up with this on your own. Let us know so we can fuck with you all season. Everyone, please make a suggestion on where you think the Muffin Man came up with this team name.

Grizz, what the hell were you thinking going to Alaska during the off-season? Heard you were up there pounding Eskimo pussy to keep warm, so you say. I heard you liked it except for the whale fat that was rotting between her teeth that made her mouth smell like the crotch of a hooker's nylons after an eighteen-hour shift with no shower. That is nasty. What the hell is wrong with you? You went up there to hunt polar bears, and the only thing you tagged was a 250-pound Eskimo. It was a woman, right? Some of the guys want to know if you took a shit outside her igloo or just shit in a corner inside the igloo. I mean, I don't care, but some people want to know. Anyway, don't forget to get your picks in this week and send Gandy a postcard. He misses you.

Mr. Gandy, I heard your mom kicked you out of the basement because the Oompa-Loompas were migrating upstairs, and she caught them sleeping in her bed and eating all the Cheetos. You know they eat those to keep that nice orange glow. The story I heard was you were sleeping in the park, covered up with newspapers for a blanket, and the other day, a squirrel came by and pissed in your ear. Is that true? You need to get a job. No, managing a fantasy football team is not a real job. I heard Chick-fil-A is hiring. Of course, you will need to wash the squirrel piss out of your ear and put on something beside a tube top and a fruit basket hat. Let us know if we can help.

Never let the Griz near your ears with his pants down.

Commish out.

Another week

Week 2 is in the books, and it looks like it was a sad week for most of us. Looks like Labia got the win this week. I cannot describe how much it pains me to have to give him the money. Still not as tough as actually getting Joel's money for the league. Joel, you are a cheap fucker. I want to know how you actually get money out of your wallet without a cutting torch. I will be by today to clip off your nipples with a pair of fingernail clippers. Don't have the money next week and I am going to tell everyone about your secret desire for men dressed up in women's clothes.

TDUB, I still do not know what a cock waffle is. Would you care to explain it to the group? That is, of course, if you can pull your head out of Elknut's ass. Someone told me he wrapped rope around your waist and was playing with you like you were a yo-yo. If that's true, I would like to see that. I know Griz was looking for another new Olympic sport to submit to the committee.

Retod and the Vag, did you two make up? I heard you did, and all is well in fairyland. Word has it you two were spotted in the park, lying in the grass and eating grape suckers out of each other's ass-holes. That is sick, but to each his own. Too much? Get over it, and remember, you are the sick ones, and I just write what I hear. Sack Attack said he wants a grape sucker.

Muffin Man, is that the best you can do? Looks like you need to stick to making and fucking muffins, and I don't mean your cat you named Muffins.

Grape Ape said he has a few things to say, but as usual, he wants to say it in a poem.

> Just wanted to let you all know
> This is my year
> I will beat Retod and the Vag
> And yes, it is because they are queer
>
> I want all the money
> And yes, I mean every penny
> But I would settle for all the money
> Put in by Vinny

Zombie, WTF! You are beating me again. Someone must be helping you, but I know it isn't Griz. So who is it? I may have to move your picks around next week.

Griz, here we go again. You have to be the only person alive that could get arrested for shitting outside in Alaska. How in the fuck can that happen? I didn't even know they had indoor plumbing. I mean, for fuck's sake, it couldn't have offended anyone. There's only forty-seven people in the whole state. You managed to drop your insulated coveralls, take off your big puffy coat, open the back flap on your long underwear (we all know that flap has a dual purpose), and shit in front of the only cop in the whole state. And I heard your defense was that the pastor of your church in Montana lets you shit out back behind the church and offered the cop the pastor's phone number to verify your story. I did see the picture from the cop car camera and laughed my ass off. It appears that your Eskimo girl-friend was standing right beside you in her winter parka with the furry hood pulled over her face so we couldn't see her. She had a stick going through the tube in the middle of the toilet paper roll. She was standing there all stiff with her arms stretched out so you could reach the roll, and she was not moving, like she was a statue. You probably wondered why she was doing that and not saying anything. That's because the cop was her dad. I have some advice for you: Start shitting in a toilet.

Mr. Gandy, I see you got out of the park and found a halfway house for you and your pet Oompa-Loompas. I did talk to the person in charge of that house, and he has some concerns. He said the Oompas were staying under your bed, and because your bed was in the living room, it was creepy because all anyone saw of them was their eyes peering out at others in the room. Most residents won't even come in there and watch TV because of those creepy little fuckers. One lady said she was eating Cheetos, and when she dropped one, it got ugly. She tried to pick it up and got bit by one of your Oompas. She said the little Oompa was quick as lightning coming from under your bed to bite her, grab the Cheetos, and scurry back under the bed. She said, "Ain't nobody got time for that." You might want to keep them in a cage or you will be on the street again.

That's it for this week. If I didn't insult you this week, don't worry, I will. None of you are safe.

Fuck you.

Commish out.

Week 3

Jokie, we have not checked in with you in a while. Let's see what you have been up to. Looks like you are leading the league with points but still don't have a win under your belt. Maybe you could concentrate better if you weren't at the homeless shelter fucking pregnant women. You know that's nasty, right? I hear the wife kicked you out because she caught you watching midget porn. Is that true? I am beginning to get a little worried about you. Have you been hanging out with Gandy? Anyway, try to keep your mind on football instead of your balls bouncing off some tiny, little midget's ass. I will check back with you next week to see if you have cleaned up your act or at least washed off your junk from the women in the homeless shelter. You know they don't bathe, right?

TPUD says he wants to apologize for anything he has said that offended anyone. I know for a fact that he isn't sorry and is just worried that if they nominate him for mayor of Shitsville, he won't get elected. Never mind all the weed he smoked, and if you lived around here, he was probably growing weed in your backyard when he was a kid.

Sack Attack (Joel), what the fuck is with the holding hands and skipping shit? Have you been ass raped by the Muffin Man again? The vegan shit is gay. Elkfag read me something about vegans. It said, "I shot a cow today because it was eating your food. You're welcome." Since it sounds like you may have a little vegan in you (along with Muffin Man's muffin top). You may want to thank meat eaters for destroying the very thing that is destroying your food source. Anyway, there is no room in this league for all that kumbaya shit. Stick to football, you little homo, and let me know if you want to press charges on the Muffin Man for the ass rape. Just remember, he has a video of you looking over your shoulder at him and smiling. If you turn the sound way up, you can hear you beeping like you were backing up a big truck. So keep that in mind, and when you vote in November, it better be red or the whole league is going to your ass, whether you like it or not.

Retod and the Vag, it looks like you two are doing good in the pool this year. Retod, you are in fifth, and Vag, you are in eleventh. I am in tenth. The only thing I don't like about that is being between you two in any way. Especially with Retod on top, as I hear he is not gentle in any way. That was information I did not need to know, Vag, but thanks anyway.

Perksmylittle Ponies, what the fuck are you doing this year? Do you see where you are in the poll? Are you trying to match Vtech in losing this year? Old Dominion? WTF? Anyway, you need to get your shit together. Maybe you need to take the Oscar Meyer wiener mobile out on tour again this year. Maybe go to a few games and pick up some info on who to pick. Either way, there is no reason to be drowning in your loserish ways with old Natty lite beer. Keep it up, and you will be able to shit through a keyhole and not spill a drop.

Grape Ape, WTF! Where are you at, man? Missing picks, getting them wrong, and eating popsicles like they are a dick. I did not get a poem from you this week. Let's work on that for next week.

Gandy, I see you are on the streets again and off your meds. I got a call from the county sheriff's office, and he wanted to know if I could come get you. I asked him what you were wearing, which he thought was odd. I explained to him that depending on what you are wearing goes to your state of mind. I told him if you were wearing a green Carhartt winter jacket, diving fins, pink leggings, and a leopard-spotted G-string, then the answer was no. That meant you were off your meds and riding the city bus again, all day, and harassing passengers. Especially that little old lady whom you asked, "If a clown fucks you in the ass and doesn't give you a reach around, is it still funny? Or does he have to give you a reach around to make it funny?" Call me so I can try to get you some medication.

Grizzlenuts, at the time I write this week, I sure hope you found a toilet to shit in. I hear you had little Lane Brooks out on the town and got him all fucked up. You know he is only twenty, right? Anyway, he called his mom all upset because you had him behind the church last night, trying to make him shit outside. Stop the shit. Shit in a toilet, and don't make other people as sick as you. Next time you go to Alaska, take Lane Brooks with you, as he is in dire need of some pussy. Maybe you could share that whale blubber—eating Eskimo whore of yours or your chiclet-toothed skank from the mini-mart gas station and laundry facilities.

That's it this week.
So until next week.
Have a blessed day.
Commish out.

Another week

Another week is in the books, and one of our rookies took the money this week. Congrats and a giant fuck you to you. Looking a little tight this year, unlike the Muffin Man's bunghole. There is only thirty-eight points separating first place from twelfth place. The nice thing about that is Elknuts is way down the list. His excuse is he was in the hospital getting a rib or two removed so he can suck his own cock. That way, he won't have to leave the house looking for whores and can concentrate on football and maybe pick a winner from time to time. I probably violated some HIPAA law about disclosure, but as you can tell, I don't give a shit.

Jokie, I see your Hokies got a win last week. Let me just tell you one thing. I don't give a shit. They got their balls handed to them by ODU. You can't wash that one off, as it will be like a case of ten-year herpes. Anyway, enough about a fictional Hokie character. Let's talk about you being in first place. Always a bridesmaid and never a bride. You can get in first place for the season overall but can't win the week outright. You must be a Hokie. Some of the other members wanted to know if you have washed off your junk from the pregnant meth heads. One of them has a pregnant wife and wants to know if you will come service her so he doesn't have to. Anyway, good luck this week, and I hope you don't get genital warts because they look fucking nasty. Kind of like those pumpkins outside Kroger. You know the ones I mean.

Carress the Websters, fuck you in the eyehole.

Grape Ape (Vanilla Gorilla), where the fuck have you been this year? I hear you talking in the hallways but not showing up for the games. Don't tell me you are too busy eating bananas and fucking chickens to get your picks in. How about a poem:

> I know I have been busy
> I try to get my picks in
> But each week it gets harder
> With TPUD's nuts on my chin
>
> I will try to do better
> Is all I can say
> At least my name is not Muffin Man
> Is that dude really gay

I am ahead of a few people
But not to many
What hurts the most is
I am behind Vinny

That's it for this week's poem
Now fuck off and leave me alone

Retod and the Vag, let's see what you two are up to this week. I see you two put on your vagina uniforms and were protesting with the other liberals at the Judge Kavanaugh hearings. Stop the bullshit, as you are making us all look bad. Can't you stick to holding hands and cornholing each other in a park somewhere or better yet at your house? Leave that man alone. He is innocent.

Gandy, well, well, well, I see you are up to your old tricks again. I thought we had gotten through all this. I hear you were riding the city bus again wearing a bright yellow snorkel and mask, a red long-sleeved flannel shirt with the sleeves cut off, a pair of brown cutoff corduroy pants, and ski boots. You also had your old friend riding the bus with you. A life-size cardboard cutout of Leonard Nimoy (Spock). Some of the other passengers heard you talking to him like he was real. You were saying things like "You better shut your mouth, Spock, or I will rip off your head and use it for toilet paper." One of the most disturbing was "No, Spock, I will not suck your cardboard dick on this bus in public. Are you sick or something?" I am no doctor, but it sounds like you may be off your meds. Get your shit together, man.

Grizzlemcfucknuts, I hope all is well with you and your gang of shit bandits. I hear you decided to take up hang gliding again. That would be a step above Hula bowling in the city park or at your grandson's show-and-tell at school. The problem is your age. Not that you are too old to do it but that you are doing it naked, which gave you the idea for your new sport—hang glider bowling. Stay with me, people, as I tell you about the new sport.

1. You need a hang glider.
2. You need a little bit of wind, which helps, but not too much.

3. You need ten bowling pins.
4. You need about one hundred yards cleared in front of the pins.
5. You need to get naked.
6. You need to get airborne.
7. You need to pick your nuts up in one hand.
8. You need to approach the pins at a low altitude. (Age plays a factor here; the older you are, the higher off the ground you will want to be. Anyone over fifty understands that.)
9. You need to drop your nuts, right before you approach the pins, to knock the pins over.
10. You may feel soreness, and because of that, the game only lasts five frames.

Grizz wants to invite everyone over for a game, if you are feeling lucky and have a hang glider. Just give him a call.

Until next week.

Fuck off and eat a dick.

Commish out.

Another week

Well, here we are again at the end of another week, and I still have not won any money. I can tell you I am not too happy about that, so I am going to kick Elkdawg in the nuts to make me feel better.

Little tidbit of information about Retod and the Vag. Not that this has anything to do with anything. But I saw R and V at a Zack Brown concert. Not a big deal, right? So I was listening to the music and minding my own business, and I looked down into the pit where people were standing to listen to the concert, and I saw that Retod was eating Cheetos. Still no big deal, right? Then I saw Retod wipe his fingers on the Vag's ass, and I noticed his whole ass was orange from where Retod had been wiping his hands on the Vag's ass. It looked like he must be on his third family-sized bag of Cheetos, judging by the amount of orange Cheetos dust on his ass. Then I noticed Retod was laughing every time he wiped his fingers on V's ass because Vag just looked at Retod like he was being affectionate (gross) and smiled. Then I noticed a sign that the Vag must have put on Retod's back. It had an arrow pointing at his ass, and it said, "Boner Garage. Everyone welcome." I laughed and threw up in my mouth a little.

Caressthewebsters, I see you won the money again. I see you are not in town, so I spent your money on beer and pussy for Gandy because he needed it. You have to collect your money by Wednesday or you lose it. I know you won't be back for a while, so I spent it. Good luck next week, and may a centipede crawl up your peehole while you sleep.

Jokie is slipping down the ladder a bit. Does it have anything to do with your onset of genital warts? I heard they can be painful but have not experienced it myself. Grizzlenuts asked me to extend an invitation to you to participate in some hang glider bowling. He said you have to bring your own balls, but you can use his glider and bottle of salve after the match. I think he just wants to see your nuts. Don't let him touch you.

Grape Ape, the commish, got a call from the gorillas in the mist-looking motherfucker during the games, and he thought he was going to win the big jackpot. Of course, three minutes later, all his dreams were crushed when Miami beat the Bears. Here is a little poem for you:

> I know you were excited
> Looking at taking home the big pot
> Who wouldn't be
> It really is a lot
>
> You thought you had it in the bag
> But then the Dolphins treated the Bears like a fag
>
> They jammed it in their asshole
> When they made that final field goal
>
> Don't worry, the money is still there
> Unlike all your hair

You always have next week to try and win
Of course, I think you will just end up with
Elknuts on your chin

Gandy, I'm glad to hear you are not terrorizing the city bus driver anymore. I am sure he appreciates it. Although I can tell you are still off your meds. I see on YouTube you were in the park selling ice cream. I am not sure where you got the ice cream cart, but I hope you did not steal it. The PETA people are pissed because you are selling squirrel ice cream. You cannot just freeze squirrels, put them in a container, and sell them as ice cream. Are you Retodded or something? You need to quit hanging out with those little orange fuckers.

Grizzlemcfucknuts, I hear your glider bowling is catching on at the old folks' home in your little town in Kansas. Not sure how you are getting all those old fuckers on gliders, but oh well. I did hear the old women were pissed because you said you had to be a man to bowl. I applaud you for extending the game to the women. I guess it would be a little easier for them with those big old saggy titties to knock the pins down. That must be a sight to see. You truly are an innovator, a sick motherfucker. But it's still nice to see someone with an imagination. Does every sport have to be about bowling? I would mention football, but it appears you should stick to bowling. Keep your fingers out of your asshole in public. I am tired of seeing you on YouTube.

That's it for this week.

Blow me.

Commish out.

Another week

Another week is in the books, and unfortunately, Vinny I Like Elknuts in My Mouth has won. This happened way too much last season, so we all need to step up and whip his elk-humping ass.

Of course, Drew was right there with him, just like last year. I think maybe they are doing their picks together when they wake up in the morning while sharing a morning cup of coffee. Don't ask, don't tell, right?

Cuppy started out near the bottom unlike last season. Let's keep it that way. I cannot have you beating me.

Grizzle nuts is always just ahead of me. I find that very irritating, and if you keep it up, I am going to have to tell the doctor at the psych ward that we let you out at nights to make your picks and that your left nut is swollen to the size of a baseball and you would love that square needle shot right in the center of your nut again. Think about that shot and get back to me. In the meantime, please make sure you are taking your meds, as I am tired of bailing you out of jail for licking people's living room windows. That is very disturbing and scares the shit out of people when they see your big, thick tongue on the window. I keep telling you there is no flavoring on them. I cannot spray every window in town with cherry flavoring. Just play with your Legos and make your picks.

Crushthewebsters, um, I don't think so because I am better than you and my brother aka "Rainman" is better than you. Shit, even my daughter whipped your ass. Nice try, though. Keep up the losing. We like it.

Jimmy V., shame on you. What the hell happened?

I will write more next week. Until then, don't forget to make your picks, and if you see Grizzlenuts, make sure to wave. He likes that.

Never run with scissors or use them to hold your dick when you piss. You never know when some asshole is going to come in while you are pissing and slap you on the back.

Commish out.

Another week

Another week is in the books, and a Webster won the money, so Elknuts can take a suck out of my mud whistle, and Crush the Websters can take a back seat where he got his first loving from a boy named Frank. Don't worry, we won't tell. What happens in the House of Asses, stays in the House of Asses.

It does still pain me to see Elknuts still in the season lead. I think I would rather chew on thumbtacks than see his name at the top of the list.

I see a couple of bottom dwellers climbed into the top five for the week. Don't worry, it will be short-lived, my little douchebags. It will be back under the porch with you for this coming week. Don't worry, we will feed you scraps like we always do.

Grizzlenuts, how is that left nut treating you? I guess I am going to have to kick you right square in the right nut if you keep doing better than I do. You know I hate that. I did speak to your doctor, and he is going to up your meds, so you will be drooling all the time. Just quit trying to sing because it is attracting squirrels, and with your hospital gown always being open in the front, you know what they are looking for. They are looking for that big swollen left nut that they consider the Holy Grail. I will do your picks for this week, and for fuck's sake, quit licking the water fountain nozzle. It is pissing people off. I brought you a case of water last week. Drink that. And no more sucking on the water fountain. I will be by next week to melt some jolly ranchers on the floor so you have something to do by licking them up. I know you like that, but the janitor hates it.

Looks like it was a rough week for the whole league. Some of us more than others, like Maggi, Tyree, and the Corn Hole.

Coopz, I can't believe you only put one point on your Packers. Don't be such a puss, or maybe you are a Vikings fan at heart. Either way, get off the babysitter.

Perks ponies, WTF! I thought you would be better at this, but I guess you just suck at it. You must be a Tech fan.

Maggi, it looks like you better put a rubber band around your head and snap the fuck out of it. Are there any lights down there in the basement? Just wanted to let you know that you suck.

That's it for this week. I will write more next week. If you have thin skin or don't like the f-word, then you may want to join a church league. Good luck this week (I don't mean that), assholes.

Blow me.

Commish out.

Another week

Another week is in the books, and with a heavy heart, I have to announce that Blow the Websters won the money this week. On a happier note, I see that Elknuts is way down the list where he belongs. I have been asked by some of you why I don't say anything about me losing. Well, it's because I am doing the writing, you fucking morons. Feel free to give me shit. I can take it, and it makes this more worth reading, so if you feel like you want to jump in and write about me, feel free to do so. Just don't go crying to your mama when I slam you back. It is all in good fun. If you can't handle it, maybe you should get a job at the circus cleaning up elephant shit.

Looks like Grizzlenuts has taken the lead for the season, but that will be short-lived. I heard you were headed up to Montana to reacquaint yourself with your squirrel friends. Don't forget what they did to your nuts last time when you fell asleep in your broken-down, dungy-brown, and one-arm-missing recliner. I hear you are still taking medicine for that. I did get a call from the pastor of the church up there when he heard you were coming. He asked me to tell you that he will not tolerate you riding your snowmobile over to the church every day and taking a shit behind the church. Anyway, good luck with the squirrels, and for hell's sake, just shit in your own toilet.

Retodd, being a Patriot's fan, I am sure you are cheating somehow to stay ahead of me or anyone else in the league, for that matter. Keep it up, and you will need to be ordering some lube off the Adam and Eve website.

Littledickbrooks, I am going to punch you in the neck when I see you, just because you are beating me.

Coop, I was expecting you to do better, but I guess your mind is on doing the nasty in the back of the new race car you bought. Get your head (the one with a face) back in the game and beat Elknuts's and Grizzlenuts's asses.

Looking for 5 dicks, you are going to need more points than that to get in the lead. Maybe it should be looking for one hundred.

The rest of you who I am beating, all I can say is "Losers."

That's it for this week. Hope you like the write-up, but if not, please feel free to go fuck yourself. Have a great and safe day. End of comment.

Commish out.

Another week

Another week is in the books, and though I thought the House of Asses would be immune to cheating, like the Patriots do, to win every week, I am saddened to say that a Patriots fan has cheated to win this week. His name is Retodd, and he is a Patriots fan. I hate to say this, but the punishment in the House of Asses for cheating is a beating with a 1970s tube sock with the green stripes at the top, filled with family-sized bars of Irish Spring still in the box. I say we beat him until all the corners are rounded on the boxes and then strip him of his twenty-five bucks. Please join me in this beating, and if you don't have the stomach for it, then maybe you need to get off your mama's titty and be a man.

Little Dick Brooks, too bad he cheated to win. The money should be yours, but you need to learn to lose like a man and not use this as an excuse to quit school and bury your fingers two knuckles deep in your ass all day while repeating, "I should have won. I should have won." Get over it, pull your fingers out of your ass, and make your picks for next week.

Grizzlenuts, looks like you are still in the lead, and you know how much I hate that. I am slipping down the ladder, and you are on top. The pastor from the church called and wanted to say thank you for not shitting behind the church. He did, however, ask me to tell you not to wear assless chaps to Sunday school, especially when you are teaching the little kids about our Lord and Savior. One of the kids is having nightmares from when you turned around and bent at the waist to pick up a crayon. His parents do not appreciate that the image of your balloon knot is imprinted on their child's brain for the rest of his life.

Coop, getting close. Always a bridesmaid but never a bride. Still no excuse to put on makeup and a skirt with no underwear on and drive the handicap cart around Walmart.

Elknuts, nice to see you down in sixth place. I guess your luck has run out. I thought the genie told you it only lasted so long, and you would have to fuck the goat again.

Jimmy Vag, I see I am beating you, and that is the part I like. The part I don't like is I have seen you hanging out with Retodd and was hoping we would not have to Irish Spring your ass next week.

That's it for this week for the House of Asses. Get your picks in and fuck off. I hope you all lose. See you all next week.

Remember, bad pussy is still pussy.

Commish out.

Another week

Another week is over, and I am not sure everyone knows this, but the winner is not even a football guy. He is a cheerleader, which makes us all look bad, especially you, Looking for5dicks. If it happens again, I guess I will have to seek the advice of Re-Todd and start cheating. Anyway, I only have one thing to say to the cheerleader, which is now your new name. Fuck you, princess. I hope you lose this week.

Lookingfor5dicks sounds like a gay Indian name. I can hear it now. Hi, my name is Lookingfor5dicks, and before you ask, no, four won't do, but any color will—black, white, or blue. I can assure you I was not drinking donkey sperm, but I was thinking that you were probably humming the song "I want to be like Mike," while you were trying to be funny. I can also assure you it does not take courage to write this shit down, which is painfully obvious because you actually put a couple of amusing sentences together. Not really funny, but it was a nice try for a gay left-handed crossdresser. Please keep the insults coming, as I like it and it gives me something to comment on. And don't worry, little buddy, someday you may even be funny if you keep trying.

Grizzlenuts, you were one game away from losing the season lead, but I guess you probably already knew that since you have nothing to do except sit around and watch old *Oprah* reruns. You know that lady that works at the convenience store around the corner from your house? You know, the one who has the greasy hair, has one big chicklet-looking tooth she had whitened (not sure why someone with one tooth would get it whitened), weighs about eighty pounds, and smokes nonfiltered Pall Malls? Anyway, she said she wants her panties back. She saw you outside your house in a 1970s lawn chair wearing a cowboy hat and her panties and nothing else while spraying some kid in a kiddie pool and feeding him Lucky Charms. Anyway, she thinks you may be stretching them out, and she only has two pairs. I don't even want to know how you got them. Should I tell her she can have them back?

RETODD is climbing the ladder just like the Patriots do, but I am keeping an eye out because I am sure you are cheating, just like the Patriots do, and we will catch you, and when we do, we are going to punch you right in the neck. I heard you went to a game last week and got put in the stadium jail for being drunk. They said you were shouting something like "Tom Brady is not a cheater. Everyone is just jealous. And I love him and want to have his babies." Then you threw up two hotdogs, a cheeseburger, some nachos, and a load of Tom's jizz on the gay couple sitting in front of you. That was when the cops came and took you away.

Perksmylittleponies, just pathetic. Not sure what else to say except get your shit together and quit playing with your pony.

Jimmy Vag, really? Enough said!

Elknuts, wow! You are sucking worse than me, but at least I am still ahead of the cheerleader. I think the ATM is closed for you. You are so far away from it you probably can't even see it if you squint your eyes. I heard you were writing a sports column in the *Appomattox Times* on how to lose at pool host.

Well, that's it for this week from the Commish. The rest of you should grow some balls like Lookingfor5dicks and insult me or at least give me shit. Please don't take any of the shit I write personal. It is just for a laugh, and if you don't think it is funny, then don't read it and go fuck yourself.

Have a nice day, assholes. Until next time. This is the Commish, saying "I hope your dog does not get ass raped by a rhino."

Commish out.

Another week

The week is over, and I will start by answering some of the comments from you fellow so-called writers.

Elknuts in Mouth is your new Indian name, by the way. Not sure you would even be able to see me through Louie's man bush in your face, looking up weather reports in the OCC, but to answer your question, yes, I am. Have you seen my picks? The ATM has always been open with your money in it, and from the looks of it, you won't be seeing any of it.

JScruggs (Pom-Poms), I'm not sure what my standings have to do with your roasting, but rest assured that the roastings will continue no matter where I am at in the standings. You just need to hope that your luck holds out because we all know you have been lucky to this point and would rather be cheering than watching football. I am not judging you, and I am sure no one cares what you put in your mouth. I guess we will see this week if you have been lucky or if your spankies were just on too tight and you got lucky.

Not sure what this league is coming to, but it looks like we are being led by a Re-Todd for the season, and a cheerleader has been climbing the ranks, no pun intended, while Grizzlenuts and Elknuts in Mouth have been falling down the ladder. Not sure what is happening, but I do not like it, especially since I am losing so bad.

Re-Todd, I could really use some tips on cheating.

Grizzlenuts, I heard a disturbing story today about you and the chicklet-toothed lady. It was a story about how you met, and I am not sure my life will ever be the same or I will even be able to look at you the same. So the story goes that you met her while she was in a ditch with clothes that are torn and weathered with that same nasty and greasy hair; dirt under the fingernails; only one shoe, which is why she walks with a limp because it is a high heel; and heels cracked and bleeding. And she didn't appear to be breathing. Basically, she was looking like the last rose of summer. The next part is the worst, which is best described by the poem you have written for your beloved. Here it goes:

> I fucked a dead whore on the side of the road
> You knew right away she was dead
> The skin on her belly was rotting
> She had nary a hair on her head
> And when my terrible deed was done
> I realized my terrible sin
> So I put my lips to her asshole
> And sucked out the wad I had shot in

Now I know we were raised in the same house, but I have to think we at least have different dads. Man, you are one sick fuck. I heard you were going to a poetry reading later this week at the old folks' home. May I give you some advice? Keep that one in your pocket and maybe save it for the family barbecue?

Jimmy Vag, what's up with you? Pretty quiet this year and sucking worse than me, which is really bad. Maybe you should spend a little less time on the babysitter and a little more time watching football.

Luke99, rumor has it that you saddled up Perksmylittleponies and rode him all the way to Brokeback Mountain where you were going to break in a couple of stallions or was it a couple of Coors Lights. We know what you are breaking. Last time you had C-radical aka "Corn Hole" up there, he came back crying, saying he did not like you anymore. I think maybe you need to settle down, Scout Master.

Well, that's it for this week, so until next week, this is the Commish, saying, "I believe it takes a big fish to fuck a whale."

Commish out.

Pick'em 2019

What's happening? This is what's happening!

Looks like we are starting another season of pick'em football. Welcome back to the people who have been doing this year to year, and a great big fuck you to the pussies who quit. We had a handful who quit because they said, "I never win." And you have to say that with your voice sounding like a four-year-old who doesn't get his way. Oh well, fuck them in the ass with a cactus dipped in battery acid.

Welcome to the newcomers. We are glad you are here. Just a couple of things you should know. Never read my posts out loud in church as the preacher will probably tell you to get the fuck out of his church. If you are easily offended, then do not read my posts, and you may want to join a church softball team instead. Remember, it's all in fun, so if you are easily butt hurt, don't read my posts because chances are, I will give you a nickname and tear into you like a honey badger on acid or a fat guy with a five-pound bag of watermelon gummy bears.

The payouts are below, and if you have any questions, give me a call or email me. If everyone will send me their cell number, I am going to put together a group text to remind everyone on Thursday to get their picks in. You don't have to, but if you do, please don't reply to the text, just put your picks in and shut the fuck up. I don't need to hear (I already have my picks in twenty times from different people). Use your head and think a little or you will end up shitting behind your church with a crackwhore named Jenny like the Grizzlenuts has for the last five years. It's not pretty, and the last thing I need is more phone calls from public officials about you dickheads. Especially you, Mrs. Gash. Try to keep some clothes on when you are in public. Every pole you see is not a stripper pole.

Retod and the Vag, I expect a little more out of you two this year. Keep your dickskinners out of the Cheetos and quit eating corn on the cob like it's a banana. It makes you look gay. I know you are gay. You don't have to tell me that, and you don't need to advertise it either.

Glad to see Joel paid at the last second, like always. Hope you didn't have to take out a loan for that fifty dollars.

Please give each other shit on the message board and feel free to give me shit. I can take it, but be prepared to get it back. It makes it more interesting.

That's it for this week.

Blow me.

Commish out.

Week 1

Well, week 1 is over, and I did not win, so that pisses me off, but you can't win them all. I guess I will roast a couple of you in the write-up to follow. Just remember, if you get offended, I don't give a flying fuck.

Retod and the Vag, it looks like the Vag washed the Cheetos dust off his butthole and off Retod's mouth and made a few good picks. At least enough to win the first week. Hopefully, Retod isn't so jealous that he refuses to fuck Vag with the stolen dick he has tucked in his side table next to their bed. Don't answer that, Vag, because we don't want to know what happens behind closed doors at your house.

Gash, I see you are near the top, but I hear that's where you like it. You know, for a chick, you have some set of balls.

Corn Hole, close, but no cigar. You landed in third place, and I think it might be because you have the calves of an ugly third grader. Of course, it might be because you have no clue what you are doing and should maybe stick to cheerleading.

Sack Attack, like your name, I hear you have been at the tranny bars, tearing up sack and singing poems on stage like you think you are Elton John. Word has it someone saw you coming out of the bar wearing nothing but a pink thong and rubber dicks glued all over your body. You were staggering and laughing while hand in hand with some guy named Richard who had big tits and was cupping your balls. You are one sick fuck.

Jokie, how about them Hokies? Looks like they are doing as well as you are. If you need some help picking, maybe the Gash can give you some pointers, if you don't mind being on bottom.

Grape Ape, looks like you are in the middle of the pack, which is where you should be because you can't pick games. Maybe you should write us another poem.

> I am in the middle of the pack
> Just like a butthole in the crack
>
> I will probably never win
> Especially with jizz on my chin
>
> I will lose but continue to try
> And in private, I will cry
>
> I will keep picking, and in the end
> Maybe one of you fuckers will be my friend
>
> That's enough of this poem
> Sack Attack is waiting for me at home

Grizzlenuts, I hear you are at it again. Got a call from some lady named Cheryl. She said you burned down her she shed after shitting in her backyard. I wasn't sure what to say, but said I would talk to you and that I would take away your matches and tell you to shit behind the church like usual.

That's it for this week. I will slam more of you next week, so don't worry, Perk's My Little Ponies, I have not forgotten you.

Remember, if you eat Cheetos and then pick your nose, everybody will know.

Commish out.

Another week

Well, another week goes by, and I didn't win. Looks like I need to kick Perksmylittleponies in the balls to make me feel better, and maybe it will bring me some good luck.

Retod and the Vag, I guess Retod pulling that dick out of your ass and making a popping sound didn't help you this week. You both ended up in the loser column. Maybe you should stick to soft porn in the city park in San Francisco. You two are sick and should be punished.

Jokie, it looks like you collected the cash this week. Maybe you can buy your wife something nice, like gas station flowers or chocolates. I think it was all luck anyway. Don't believe those people who say you are stupid because you are a Hokie fan. The world needs ditch diggers, too, and with your engineering degree from Tech, you could be lead digger. Just saying, you may as well use that degree.

Grape Ape, it looks like you are hanging near the top. I will share your latest poem, if you don't mind, and fuck you in the face, if you do mind.

> I'm Grape Ape
> Hanging near the top
> Those of you below me
> Can eat my ass like pig slop
>
> If you don't like me
> I don't care
> You can tongue my balls
> And lick my ass hair
>
> I'm near the top
> That is where I will stay
> Fuck Retod and the Vag
> Those dudes are totally gay
>
> That's it for now
> It's the end of the poem
> I need to drop off my girlfriend
> 'Cause my family is waiting for me at home

Gash, what the fuck? I think you are doing some insider training or maybe you are "doing" the whole team. My goal is to beat you
like the sun beats a ginger in the Arizona desert.

Grizzlenuts, well, well, well. Let us see what you have been up
to. Doesn't seem like too much this week. I got no phone calls about
you, and I like that. Even though you burned down Cheryl's she
shed, she is inviting you to her barbecue to unveil your new sport
you want to get into the Olympics. She requests you wear clothes this
time, and assless chaps are not clothes. She also doesn't like clowns
with no pants because it is not funny.

That's it this week.

Please feel free to go fuck yourselves.

Commish out.

Another week

Well, it looks like I did not win again, so all I have to say is a
big happy fuck you to all of you, and I am looking to win next week.

69er, it looks like the newcomer has taken the cash this week.
Don't get used to it, or we will have to tie you up and whip that ass
like we know you like it.

Elknuts, I got some disturbing news about you today. I was kind
of sickened by what I heard and, at the same time, felt sad for you.
Word has it you were at the mall in Charlotte at the food court, fucking a midget on the merry-go-round. The innocent bystanders weren't
so much appalled at the fact that you were fucking a red-headed
midget as they were at looking at your naked ass as you pumped that
thick-fingered dwarf. When interviewed, they said the worst part was
looking at your naked ass. They said it looked like someone filled a
sock with marbles and beat your ass with it for a week straight. Why
don't you take that shit to the city park like everyone else? Maybe you
can hook up with Grizlnuts and his chicklet-toothed whore. I hear
that is where he is taking his dumps lately. Anyway, have fun in court
defending your actions. You are one sick fucker.

Grape Ape, it looks like you are the season leader. Maybe you can grace us with another one of your awesome poems.

> I am on top
> because I know how to pick
> Not sure about the rest of you
> You all must be busy sucking dick
>
> Your picks really suck
> Hopefully you are better when you fuck
>
> I also plan on winning
> This coming week
> So pucker up your lips
> And kiss between my cheeks
>
> No more needs to be said
> I will be taking more money and spending it on
>   getting your grandma to give me head

Grizzlenuts, what have you been up to other than filming Elknuts at the mall in Charlotte? I hear you have been sitting outside Starbucks, throwing hot coffee on Bernie Sanders fans. I applaud you. Keep up the good work and try to lay off the twinkies. They are making your ankles fat.

Another week

As usual, I lost. What is more painful than losing is that Elknuts won and that makes me want to throw up and kick him in the balls with steel-toed shoes on fresh out of the freezer.

Hey, 69er, Reloader has your cash, so make sure he does not skip town on you or hit any strip bars, or you won't see your money. Just saying, he has been known to show up to work wreaking of booze with glitter on his face and all over the front of his pants.

Retodd and the Vag, I saw you homos doing a commercial with Alex Trebek. Not bad, but I can't believe they let you say that on TV. It went like this for everyone who did not get a chance to watch it.

> We just turned sixty
> We're queer
> What's our price, Alex?
> Alex said, "$10.99 even for you."
> I laughed, but I think I prefer the old lady still

Grape Ape, I see you are still on top. Must be because of those outstanding poems you write. Let's hear another one if you got the time.

> I am on top
> For another week
> If it's my balls to lick
> Is what you seek
>
> Have no fear
> You fucking queer
> They will be right here on top of your head next
>   week
>
> If you don't like this
> Or any other poem
> Then go fuck your sister again
> She is waiting for you at home

Grizzlenuts, let's see. Where were you and what were you doing the last time we checked in with you? You were recording Elknuts fucking a redheaded, thick-fingered, and no-knee-having midget. Oh, you were practicing your new sport you want to get into the

Olympics. Okay, so I am going to share the rules of your new game with the league and see what they think. Here goes.

The game is called CornBungHole

Just like Cornhole with a few twists that are, to
tell the truth, pretty fucking sick.

Two-man teams on opposite sides

Each team has four beanbags

The team member not throwing will be, let's say,
receiving.

The receiver strips off all his clothes

Gets on all fours and points his ass at his teammate
(lying on his face and spreading his ass cheeks
is optional; you will understand in a minute)

The thrower (tosser) throws all four beanbags to
acquire as many points as possible

Here is the sick part: how to score

One point for landing the beanbag on the back
(it has to stay for all four throws to count)

Two points for grazing the nutbag and making
him flinch

Two points for a direct hit on the mud whistle
but does not stick

Three points if the tosser hits the balloon knot
and the receiver can slam his cheeks together
hard enough to catch the bag. Must hold the
bag for at least two seconds.

Play to twenty-one or until the other team gives
up. Whichever comes first.

Not sure this game is going to make it as an
Olympic sport, Grizzlenuts, but you keep
trying, little buddy.

That is it for this week. Until next time, never put your Cornbunghole bags in the freezer before a match.

Commish out.

POEMS

Poem to My Son on His Eighteenth Birthday: Eighteen and Life to Go

to Zaq

Never thought I would see it
The day you would be eighteen
I thought for sure
You would be dead or in jail as a preteen

There were some rough times
Like when you wanted to be one of the thugs
Even though you were only in eighth grade
You thought it would be cool to deal drugs

All the times you got kicked out of school
By doing things you thought would make you
    cool
Hopefully now you see
That doing stupid shit like that; you may end up
    in jail with a butt buddy

WHAT THE HELL IS WRONG WITH YOU?

One day you thought it would be nice
To grab a girl's tits and ass
You quickly found out who your friends weren't
Turns out it was the whole class

Then you got your license
Now you drive
I was scared to death
That within two weeks you would not be alive

We have had a lot of good times
Like the times when you thought you were funny
Even though we both know that if you did it for
        a living
You would make no money

I am so proud of you and your work ethic
And how you work so hard
Sometimes I just wish you would volunteer
To do a fucking dish and quit pissing in the exact
        same spot in the yard

You are about to graduate
A day I wondered if I would ever see
Now you are getting straight As
And all I can say is "Fuck me"

Now comes a very hard part for me
You want to get in the ring to fight
I am okay with that
As long as you don't get hurt, it will be a good night

You grew up so fast
Where did the time go
I am so very proud of you
Now for you, it is eighteen and life to go

Zaq's Nineteenth Birthday

Flip flap apple jack
Get your hand off your bone
Not sure why you have to do that
While you are on the throne

Not sure why that takes an hour
Which is half the time it takes you to take a fuck-
    ing shower (what are you doing in there)

Your birthday is coming soon
So we got you a six-pack of condoms
Instead of party balloons

Not to worry
They are not for other girls
They are for a couple of female flying squirrels

So you quit your first real job
Because the manual labor was so hard
And you traded it in for a job
That can be done by a tard

That was a joke
Quit acting like you are going to choke

Congratulations on your new job
Now quit dressing like a slob

Wash your ass and get a trim
For god's sake, brush your teeth, your breath
    smells like a Slim Jim

WHAT THE HELL IS WRONG WITH YOU?

Happy birthday, hope this isn't your last one
And for god's sake, don't ever let me catch you
    wearing a man bun

Happy birthday, love you

Lane at Twenty

You are no longer a teenager, which means you
    finally made it
Now you are twenty
The only thing you have to show for it is how
    you can put down some Pepsi
And I mean fucking plenty

We never know what to get you for your birthday
    as you never tell us your wishes
You better say something next year or all you are
    getting is some Betty Crocker dishes

Got a part-time job at the UPS and are waiting
    for them to call back, I guess
Kind of like waiting for that first girl to bend
    over and say yes

I hope they call you soon so you can get back
    in the truck or go to the warehouse to learn
    how to pack a box
All I know is you better do something soon or
    for money, you might end up sucking cocks

No matter what you do with your future and
    your plans
Even if you are at Taco Bell washing pans

Always be the best you can be
You do you, Lane B.

WHAT THE HELL IS WRONG WITH YOU?

Always remember and don't ever forget our love
    for you is legit
Happy birthday, and soon, I hope you get some
    tit

You just turned twenty, and I am jealous, so I
    have no pity
Please get you some pussy so you can quit jacking
    off to that National Geographic titty

That's it for this poem, there is no more
You better have a list next year or we are getting
    you an STD-infested whore

Zaq Nearly Twenty-One and Life to Go

Let's talk about Zaq and his next stage of life
Thought he was just off to the Navy, and now he
      is going to have a wife

He does not know what he is in for
Now he can't be a whore

He looks happy with that shitty smile
Hope it lasts for more than just a little while

Signed up for the Navy even though he had a job
I hope his new adventure teaches him how not
      to be a slob

His old job had him traveling, working twelves
      and being tired
Decided to act like an asshole, so as you can
      guess, he got fired
He is leaving soon for the Navy, in less than a
      week, he will be in boot camp
No more privacy for snapping his carrot by his
      little bedside lamp

He will finish boot camp and be off to ET school
      and then to be a Navy SEAL
He won't be able to be a slob there, is really how
      I feel

Just wanted to make sure you know we are proud
Not sure why when you and Lane are together,
      you are so fucking loud

WHAT THE HELL IS WRONG WITH YOU?

You know we will miss you
That includes your sister and brothers from
    another mother
No matter where you go or what you do
Know one thing, we love you

Your birthday is coming soon, life starts getting
    faster, trust me it is not slow
You will soon be twenty-one with life to go
We love you

Murder Mystery

Some of you are new to this murder mystery shit
    and should know that we start out with a
    poem
If you don't like it or you are bored, feel free to
    put a cheek in each hand and carry your ass
    home

Polly Abdool looking like an eighty's chick
I seen you staring at Nork's massive dick

Nork from Pork looking like a mass-murdering
    douche
Are you sure you should be on the loose

Toni Oregano are you sure that's eighties attire
I heard that Dundee fucker wants to put more
    than air in your rear tire

Debbie Gribson you eighties-looking punk
Nozzie Nozborne is spreading the word that you
    have a lot more than junk in your trunk
    (dead body)

Dannyson, you karate-chopping murdering little
    geek
Howard Scott said you were packing, so open up
    that kimono and give us a little peek

Lindy Lauper, I see you are all decked out like
    you are from the eighties, complete with
    that pouty lip
Just remember you were actually born in the fifties,
    so make sure you are holding on to something;
    we wouldn't want you to fall and break a hip

Alligator Dundee from the eighties and packing
  a huge knife
We were all wondering how you disposed of the
  dead body of your wife
Some say you burned her and some say you bur-
  ied her alive
Some say you ate her, but I think you fed her to
  an alligator for dinner at five
David Bouie all decked out with your frilly
  clothes and makeup and not knowing people are staring or you don't care
You might feel different if you knew your pants
  had a split in them and they have to look at
  your ass hair
Would it be too much to ask you to put on some
  fucking underwear

Nozzy Nozborne, you freaky-looking, bat-biting
  punk
If you kill anyone at this party, you will be the
  one in Debbie Gribson's trunk

Howard Scott, guess it's nice not to have to dress
  up for the part
If you bite anyone at this party tonight, your
  dead ass will be dragged out of here on a cart

That's it for this poem, so let's get this party
  started and have some fun
And for god's sake, Dannyson, learn to pull out
  before you cum.

For You Two

I remember when Marysa was born, I was a long
    way out of town
I drove a thousand miles straight just to see her
    face, and of course, it was a smile and not a
    frown

As she grew, she was my pride and joy
Never asking for a girl's toy
Didn't want Barbies or kitchen sets with pots and
    pans
She looked up at me and said, for my birthday, I
    want a deck of cards, dice, and a garbage can
She never got into too much trouble
It's not because I kept her like the boy in the plas-
    tic bubble

There were times she even got her ass beat
And it was for more than not keeping her room
    neat

Then comes a scary part where she learned to
    drive
She only hit one guard rail but always came home
    alive

Then it comes time to date
And as a father, we all know we don't want to
    open that fucking gate

But of course, we have no choice she had to date
    one with a big head who might be gay
And one so small with one nut that his parents
    should have been feeding him hay

WHAT THE HELL IS WRONG WITH YOU?

She went through a bad breakup or two, but hav-
    en't we all
So glad they are not in your life because between
    the two of them, I bet they didn't have one ball

Of course, everything happens for a reason, and I
    believe you went through all this
So you would be prepared for your soulmate, Chris

Chris, don't think for one second that I left you
    out of this poem
Our family welcomes your sweet little ass to our
    home

Marysa told us we would love you from the start
She was right, and we knew you were family when
    you let go of that first nasty fart (joking)

I am sure you weren't perfect and got a beating
    or two
Good fucking thing is, it means your parents love
    you

I am sure you also went on a date or three
I just hope you took care of that burning when
    you pee

I can't tell you how happy we are that you and
    Marysa met
Pretty sure you all feel the same way, I bet

Since this is dragging on and everyone is proba-
    bly getting bored
I should end this poem and be done
By saying we love you both, and don't look at it
    like we are losing a daughter but gaining a son

Webster 2017 Christmas Poem

Thought I would start a new tradition for the
    Webster Christmas and write a poem
Maybe to cover the years activities at our home

I will cover each person in the family as to what
    they have done
Some might be bad and some might be fun

There may be some words that make you want
    to cry
Suck it up buttercup 'cause you won't die

Teri started her year in the lunch lady field
Had to quit that because what sucked was the
    yield
So now if you need her, she will come clean your
    house
Just make sure she won't see a mouse

She finally got a new kitchen
Even paint and wallpaper on the walls
Now just maybe when it comes to the kitchen
She will quit busting my balls

Next comes Marysa, not sure what to say
Had a rough spot, but at least she's not gay

She did something I never thought she would do
Got herself a beautiful white dog
And now she is cleaning up piss and poo

Finally got to spend a little time in the house she
    built
I know Steve is over there in a skirt

WHAT THE HELL IS WRONG WITH YOU?

You can't hide that fact by calling it a kilt

I know she hates it, but now she has a yard to
    mow
Begs her brother to do it
But of course, he says fuck, no

Got a little sick at the end of the year
Got a case of the shingles is what I hear
I hate to shingle her out
But I hear it will make you more than pout

Next comes Lane, and he had a big year
Jury is still out on if he is queer

Before you get all ass hurt and start to pout
I know you like naked girls, of that, I have no
    doubt

You finally finished your high school career
And amazingly enough, you had your first beer

I know we were in your ass about a career
But when we asked you, you just shrugged your
    shoulders and said have no fear

Sometimes when we asked you got a little bent
Along came September, and you still had no
    income to pay the rent
All we heard was I am waiting and hoping UPS
    calls
All I know is, with all that ass mashing, you must
    have one sore set of balls

Glory halla-fucking-lua, the call from UPS finally
	came
At the end of November, they called your name
Now we see you in the brown UPS truck sitting
	all tall
Looking like a creepy, chucky bobblehead doll
Looks like you are on the right path
Even though you suck at English and Math

Next comes Zaqariah double chin
Sometimes we don't want to admit it, but we love
	him and he is our kin

Looks like you got tired of building that bridge
	across the road
Got a job at Areva and going to college
Finally, carrying an adult workload

Got yourself a nice little bachelor pad
But I have seen some of the skanks you bring
	there, and it is sad

Seems on your time off, all you do is hunt and
	fish
There is one thing that I wish
That you shave that ball sack hair off your face
You look so much better without it and besides
	having ball hair there, is out of place

Got yourself a nice brand-new ride
Got rid of the truck, so now you don't have to
	hide
Got yourself a pretty little cat
Went on the road and came back fucking fat

WHAT THE HELL IS WRONG WITH YOU?

I told you some day you would see
You would end up fat like me

Next comes Brady
I think sometimes he wants to be a lady

Just joking, I know he likes girls
For some reason, he doesn't like wildlife because
    I hear him singing, "Daddy, please don't take
    the squirrels"

All you do twenty-four seven is play basketball
And of course, wish you were seven feet tall
This was your year for getting tall
We measured you with your back to the wall

Every time against the wall your ass would park
We would look at it and have to raise the mark
I swear you grew six inches more
Than the first time this year we put your back to
    the door

I am starting to worry you might be a girl
Every day you want a new pair of shoes with that
    Nike Swoosh

The weird thing is they are not to put on and
    dance
You just leave them in the box, and every once in
    a while, you give them a glance

That's it, the end of the poem
Now all you fuckers go home

Just joking, you all know you are welcome here
We like having you but not enough to cheer

We say Merry Christmas in this house and believe
    Jesus is Lord
But when I look out among you and think to
    myself, *Look at the one with the huge Ricky*
    Bumper head gourd

I love you all, that there is no doubt
Now for the last time, get the fuck out

2018 Webster Family Christmas Poem

Last year, we started a family tradition
So here is this year's edition

Grab your tits and grab your cocks
And just hope this year the poem rocks

If you don't like it, that's okay
It just means you are probably gay

This year, even though he is not here, I will talk
    about my brother
As you have probably guessed, we have the same
    mother

Doug has another brother and sister
Whose life I have not followed
I am guessing those are two times my mom
    should have swallowed

Doug had a rough bout with a flesh-eating virus
That thing was nasty and kind of looked like
    Miley Cyrus

It came in next to his butthole like a wrecking
    ball
At eight inches long, it was not small at all

Good news is, he is all better
Too bad he's not here to hear this letter

Because he is excited, next comes Bobby
Just don't tell his boyfriend, Robby

If you need someone to build you a home
I recommend you hire this tiny fucking gnome

Not sure why you don't build yourself a house
    and that you live in a tree
At least you don't have to go outside to pee

The tree is nice and even has a shelf
Which you need to put your cookies on
Because you really are the Keebler fucking elf

He even built me a beautiful deck
Then fell off the fucker and almost broke his neck

Just busting his balls, this is one awesome man
I just wish he would quit dressing like Peter fuck-
    ing Pan
That's it for your part
I promise not to tell anyone you shit your pants
    every time you fart

Jay, you are up next
So put down the fucking phone, this is not a text

Let's start with that—let's call it a beard
Shave that shit off, it looks fucking weird

I'm not saying it looks gay
But it does make you look like you may be full of
    white trash DNA

Now you are raising dogs and got you a Mustang
Only thing you're missing is some poontang

Just joking, stay away from the stank
That way you will have more money in the bank

WHAT THE HELL IS WRONG WITH YOU?

Of course, then there is Pam
Some might say, as gentle as a lamb

Those of us that know her know better
She will bite your hand off if you try to pet her

She is quick to light up a smoke
And will most certainly laugh at a joke

She has a pretty good life, she will tell you herself
It doesn't even bother her that she is married to
 the elf on a shelf

The one thing that makes her sad
Is her daddy's pigs, or does that make her mad

That's Pam in a nutshell
If you don't like her, you can go to hell

Dean Dean long and lean
You are a storytelling machine

I could listen to your stories all day
And no, that does not make me gay

I am ready for another one, so light up a cigar
Think of a good one, and I will meet you at the bar

Next, we have Dean's wife, Sue
I think they met over a beer and sniffing glue
That's not true, but there is a story here
One that Dean told me while having a cigar and
 a beer
She might seem a little quiet and shy
Get a few drinks in her, and she will cuss you bad
 enough to make you cry

On vacation, we were just having a drink and sit-
    ting around
She gets on Dean about smoking cigars that had
    us rolling on the ground

I don't think Dean liked it, but let's hear that one
    again
We will get her a few drinks, and he will just have
    to take it on the chin

Here comes Lane, and he has a job
But is still polishing his own nob

He finally decided what he is going to do
He wants to be an IT guru

So he is going to college for that
I just hope he doesn't start wearing a pussy hat

He is finally moving forward with his life
Maybe one day, if he isn't gay, he will get himself
    a wife

Teri, after being fired is back at the school
This time-watching little fucked-up kids drool

I know there are some that she wants to whip
    their tail
She better quit soon or she is going to kill a kid
    and end up in jail
She quit a job earlier this year and to just be blunt
It was working for a convicted felon and a lying
    fucking cunt

WHAT THE HELL IS WRONG WITH YOU?

Cody, you are next
Wishing you could beat me to the fuck-you-Fri-
    day text

A man of many talents
From a foul-mouthed welder
To Sundays where he is a church elder

Here's a guy who will give you the shirt off his
    back
And the very next instance bends over and shows
    you his ass crack
He really is a nice guy
Just don't get too close because I think he has a
    sty

Don't know what to say about Codie the girl
I have heard she has never blown a squirrel

With their new business, I can see she runs the
    show
That would make her the Mama San, not just
    another ho

Word has it she got some insurance money to get
    the business ahead
I hear it was from burning down her own fucking
    she shed

Brady is still young with nothing to lose
Just like a homo, he wants to buy nothing but shoes
He finally got one wish after all
He started to grow and is getting tall
Of that, I am glad to see
Now he doesn't have to stand on his tiptoes at the
    toilet to pee

Joey, glad to see you are here
Two kids and four girlfriends later, we know you
     are not queer
Black belt in karate and quick to sing a song
Your last girlfriend told us you have a tiny dong
I don't know if I believe her 'cause she is pretty
     sick
I do have to say, though, for a chick, she has a
     pretty big dick

Katie is here, and I hope she brought cake
That shit is good, this bitch can fucking bake
That's not why we love you and would like to see
     you more
But we know you are busy being a whore
I hope you know that's a joke
But word has it the last dick you had made you
     choke

Let's see, what I can say about me
My year was great
I had three weeks off paid, or was it eight
Just joking, it was eight
I know that makes Cody irate
All in all, it was a good year
Not that I care, but none of the boys came out
     and said they were queer
Gonna have our first grandchild
They have no idea what they are in for, but we
     know it won't be mild
Can't wait until next year, we can buy the little
     fucker presents
Unless I lose my job and we are living like peasants
That's all I have to say about me
I am awesome as you can see

WHAT THE HELL IS WRONG WITH YOU?

I hope this poem finds you jolly and you deck
the halls
If not, you can always tongue punch my balls
We welcome some newcomers to our special lit-
tle flock
Just remember, to be accepted, you have to kiss
Big Daddy's sock

That's it for this year, the poem is over
We are glad you all came
Just remember, I don't give a shit if you think the
poem was lame

I will be writing another one next year
If you are lucky enough to be in it
I am sure it will say something about you being
queer

Merry Fucking Christmas

Lane's Nineteenth Birthday

Roses are red
Your balls are blue
We can take care of that
With a Walmart shopping cart or two

Your birthday has gone by
But that is no reason to cry
You never know you just might get a date
It could even be before you graduate

Could be a girl from church or the soccer team
Might even be one from the school band
I know you don't care, as long as you can start
    using someone else's hand

Happy birthday, hope you have a lot more
And for god's sake, don't be like Zaq
And turn into a fucking whore

That's it, the end of the poem
Just one more thing
Close your bedroom door when you are snap-
    ping your carrot at home

Happy birthday, love you

My Name Is Cody, and I Am Thirty-Eight Today

Its Cody's birthday
He turns thirty-eight today
I am surprised he is still living
Being a welder and being gay

Because it's his birthday
I hope he didn't have to make his own bed
Maybe if he's lucky
His wife will give him some head

I can tell you he is one hell of a guy
He would give you the shirt off his back
But I think he needs to go to Duluth trading post
And get him some long shirts that will cover his
    ass crack

Forever trying new things
Like trying to ride a wave
That shit was hilarious
Because his shorts would not behave

The water had him spinning
And looking like a top
Then out comes the ass hair
Thinking maybe you should shave that mop

Christmas Poem 2020

It's 2020 and time for a Webster family Christmas
  poem
As usual, it will not be as mild as that Christmas
  movie *Home Alone*

Teri is first out of the gate
With who yelled like she is irate
She is a feisty little bitch
That is always ready to grapple
Then looks bewildered out in the yard
When she finds a chewed-up apple

So wrapped up in the *Yellowstone* movie
That when we were playing a game and the
  answer is supposed to be about the weather
  and asked what season is it right now
She answers with a shout, season 3

I have never known anyone
That can shit so much
If you piled it all up at the end of the day and fell
  off that pile
You just might need a crutch

Next comes Brady
Got himself a new car
Thinks he now has all this freedom
But we won't be letting him get very fucking far

Picked up golf and dropped basketball
Which is weird because now he is finally getting tall
No big deal, I guess you like what you like
I think deep down, he wants to be like Big Daddy
  Mike

WHAT THE HELL IS WRONG WITH YOU?

Not sure what is up with his hair
Not that I care
It's all curly and wild like an afro
Not sure what plans he has for that dew
But I think maybe his mom has some explaining
    to do

Lane is next, and he is still in school
Not sure how long that is going to take this tool
I am beginning to think he is going to school
With kids that drool
He is going for a two-year degree
All I can say is "Fuck me, he is twenty fucking
   three"

Doesn't drink too much or light up a cig
But if he stands sideways, he is starting to look
   like a potbelly pig
I am thinking he needs some bigger clothes
Or he could lose some weight by fucking nasty hoes

Next comes Marysa with her soda can-sized turds
I can't believe she is teaching Carter all those bad
   words
Always having a rough time at work
Be glad you are not a green alien or you might be
   getting corn holed by Captain Kirk

Not sure what got it started
Marysa told us you can get pink eye just because
   in your face someone farted

Next comes Chris and what a year
If he ain't taking a piss he is hitting a deer
A deer is what totaled his car and
I am thinking the deer may be paying him back

For shooting his brother last year just because he
    had a big rack
Got a new truck and still waiting on the call
For his new job
I think he is starting to wonder who he has to
    blow to get that call (psst, I think it's some
    fat guy named Bob)

Lucas is next, and we welcome him to our home
He likes to play with Legos, and I think I seen
    him hug a gnome
I have never seen anyone eat that many grilled
    cheeses in my life
If I did, that I would never shit again, unlike my
    wife
Lucas we are glad you are here
We are glad you are not queer
No, you can't drink a beer
Yes, your farts make my eyes tear

Zaq and Iza living overseas
I think he can still touch his dick
But I know he can't see it when he pees
Wish you weren't so far away and
For Christmas, you could be home
Shave what little hair you have left
And shine up that big dome

That's all I have from the cheermeister this year
Now one of you fuckers be a dear and get me a
    beer
I have nothing left to say or do
Except for Merry Christmas, I fucking love you

SECTION 4

I decided to start writing about all the weird shit that happened to me because when I told people the stories, they laughed and told me I should write a book. The following is a short list of what I think most of us go through. Of course, while it is happening to us, we feel like we are the only ones going through it.

- I always get screwed at the drive-through.
- My traffic lights are always longer than everyone else's.
- I always get in the slow line at the store.
- It seems like I always have to pass that slow asshole on the right because he is intent on driving five miles per hour in the fast lane, fucking asshole.
- People just come up to me and start talking. This is what really prompted me to start writing this book. Being a complete stranger, you will not believe the shit that people say to me. I will start with all the things I can remember and then try to keep track from there.

Anyway, in the following pages, I hope you will find some things that make you laugh your ass off or at least chuckle, and if they don't, fuck you.

There will also be stories from my childhood that I can remember. Some of them, I think, are funny and some are just weird or fucked up.

So here goes. The following are short stories or situations that I have encountered.

Shipping

Today I went to a place where they ship things. No, not a post office, smart-ass, like a mailbox, etc. You know, a local store, not a big chain store. Anyway, as I was giving the lady at the counter my items to mail, I started pushing the buttons on these stuffed bears at the counter that played music when you pushed the button. One of the bears was playing an Alice Cooper song, and that was when it all started.

The lady at the front desk asked me if she ever told me about the time she was at an Alice Cooper concert. I said, "No, you haven't because I have never seen you before, and we are in Oswego, New York, and I live in Lynchburg, Virginia."

So she proceeded to tell me the story. She was sitting in the front row, and Alice grabbed her by the hair and said as he was singing, "This girl is poison." She said it was the highlight of her life (she was about fifty) then started into another story about how Rod Stewart asked her sister out when they were at a concert. She wished her sister would have gone because Rod would be her brother-in-law today.

I am guessing it was her friend who also worked there, and she felt the need to tell me that she bought her grandma four of the musical bears at the counter and told me what song each bear sang. She also informed me that she would be buying Grandma more of these bears because Grandma loves them. This was the only time I had ever seen these ladies. This shit happens to me all the time.

Part of the book will be stories just like this but funnier.

Walmart and My Car

I came out of a Walmart one day pushing our usual full cart of groceries when I was stopped by an older couple. They wanted to know if I liked my Saturn outlook. Then they just broke into how they were going to buy a Saturn, and they just couldn't make up their minds between the Saturn and a Ford van. While they were rambling on and I was standing there in the heat with the fresh ice cream I just bought melting inside its container, I thought to myself, *Do I really give a shit whether they buy a car like the one I have, or better yet, do they think I give two shits what kind of car they buy?* Once again, I had never seen these people before. WTF!

Hairdo

Guess where this next one took place. You guessed it, Walmart. I went to Walmart to return an item I didn't want. So I was in the customer service area of Walmart. As I was standing in the back of the line waiting for some lady trying to return diapers, claiming they already had shit in them or maybe it was a camera, I was not sure. I saw this lady approaching me from the right. She was walking very fast with a little four-year-old blond kid in tow, almost dragging him, and she was looking very pissed and pretty rough looking. Kind of like the last rose of summer, all disheveled and hanging on by a thread. Anyway, nothing unusual happened as she was approaching me. In fact. I took a step back as she got closer to make way for her to get past me. As she was coming up to me to pass by, she turned her head and looked right at me without breaking stride and said, "I don't know what kind of hairdo I have." She turned her face back forward and walked off into the sunset, never to be heard from again, from me anyway. WTF!

Elevator Ride

This next one is about an elevator ride in the town of St. Joseph, Michigan, while doing an inspection at the Palisades Nuclear Plant. So the story goes like this.

I got back to the hotel from work one day, just like any other day. No issues. I got on the elevator that only went up four floors. Not a big hotel. As I got on the elevator, I noticed the maintenance guy for the hotel was on there. I had seen him around but had never talked to him prior to this short elevator ride. As I got on, he said hello, and I said hello back.

He said, "How are you doing?"

And I said, "I am doing great. How are you doing?"

Apparently, that was the wrong question because he unloaded on me. He told me how he was on his second marriage and that he hated his job. He was actually a certified Ford mechanic. Then he told me that his current wife had accused him of being a lazy piece of shit, and she thought that he was sexually abusing her daughter—his step-daughter. Then he told me how his real daughter flunked out of college and married a loser with no job. As weird as it might sound, he was kind of upbeat and friendly. This ride took all of fifteen seconds, and he got all that blurted out to me, a complete stranger. WTF?

Walmart Phone

This next one is better told than written, but I will do my best to paint you a picture of what actually happened and try to make it as funny written as it was in person.

It all started on Wednesday night after we dropped the kids off at youth group. The wife and myself usually went running around or shopping until it was time to pick up the kids from church. That particular night, we decided to go get some groceries. We started at Sam's Club for the items we bought in bulk. All went well in Sam's Club, as we were laughing and cutting up, just a normal night in my life. I paid, and we went out to the truck to load the groceries. As we were loading our groceries, I noticed this old man trying to stuff this huge box into the back seat of his car. A guy walked by and asked him if he needed help, and he just grumbled that he did not need any fucking help. He continued to struggle, so I decided to go help him.

I went over and asked him if he needed help, and he told me that my help was not needed. (He clearly needed help.)

I said, "Yeah, well, you are getting help anyway." I helped him, and after struggling with twisting and turning, we finally got the box in the car. He got in his car and left without a word. I thought to myself, *I hope I don't get that fucking crusty when I get old.*

We then headed to Walmart to purchase the rest of our groceries and whatever else we needed. I got a little ahead of her in the store, and I was looking at something I wanted to buy. This next part is a little hard to explain, but do you remember when you were a kid and you got some playing cards and a clothespin? You would pin the card to the frame of the bike and into the spokes of the tire so it would make a sound when you were riding your bike. You know the sound if you had ever done this. I was standing close to the shelves when she went to push the cart behind me. I turned and thrust out my pelvis at the cart, which had wires that resembled the spokes on a bike tire, like I had a chubby, and my mouth made that sound of the cards on your bike as she went by. She laughed so hard she almost pissed her pants. We got over that one and calmed down when we were done laughing. So we moved on, and when I went to twirl my phone in its pouch on my belt, like I always did, I noticed it was not there. I asked her if she had it, and she said no.

I said, "Shit, I lost my fucking phone."

So we split up and went looking for my phone. We did not find it. She said she called it, but no one answered. I said, "No shit. Did you expect me to answer it?"

Then she told me to call my phone, and I said, "With what? Do you think I might answer it this time?"

So I took her phone and tried again to call my phone to see if someone had maybe picked it up. Surprise, no one answered. Well fuck, this sucked. When I tried to close her phone, I dropped it and pieces went flying everywhere. I bent over to pick up the pieces, and my pants split from the bottom of my zipper to the top of my kneecap down the right side. She saw her phone and asked me what the fuck I was doing to her phone. I stood up and gestured to my junk spilled out all over the front of my pants, and she just burst out laughing. As I continued to pick up her phone, she kept saying, "Don't look at me."

Because she knew if I did she would laugh so hard she would piss her pants. Too late. She pissed her pants, and not just a tinkle but a full-blown grown woman's piss. So there we were, standing there with a pair of pissed pants and a pair of pants with my junk hanging out the front of my split pants. We still had a full cart of groceries we needed to pay for and a lost cell phone. Not having a very good night. Lucky for her she was wearing a long sweater that went to the back of her knees. I was not so lucky. We still had to check out and pay for our groceries. We were getting some pretty strange looks. I was thinking that it being Walmart that we blended rather nicely. All I was missing was a NASCAR jacket and a mullet to fit in there at the local Walmart. Next, we decided to head back to Sam's Club to see if anyone had turned in my cell phone. I wondered what adventure might be awaiting us there. She chose to stay in the truck with her pissed pants and made me go in alone with my shit falling out. I walked in through the double doors and strolled up to the counter and asked if anyone had turned in a cell phone but not before she looked at my junk hanging out and rolling her eyes. She then proceeded to tell me that it would be at customer service if anyone had turned it in. So as I was walking over to customer service, they all noticed my junk hanging out the front of my pants. I asked about the phone, and she treated me like I was a criminal. Anyway, I got my phone because they did have it at the counter. We then picked up the kids and told them the story, and they were rolling on the floor. They were laughing so hard.

Walmart Hawaiian Shirt

Guess where this next one happened? You are correct, Walmart. Are you starting to see a theme here? I spent a lot of time at Walmart, or it is crazy to think that every time I went there I got accosted by someone. So I was there looking at the racks full of Hawaiian shirts because I liked them and they were comfortable. This old guy in a ratty old T-shirt, cutoff jean shorts that were all frayed to hell, and what used to be white tennis shoes, came up to me to let me know I would need to go a little farther south to wear one of the shirts I was looking at. I, of course, immediately thought, *Shut the fuck up and mind your own business.* I didn't say that to him, but what I did say was you needed to get a little farther downtown toward the ghetto to be parading that ensemble around that you had on. Just once, I would like to go to Walmart and not be mind-raped by some fuck that felt the need to talk to me.

Syracuse Mall

This next one, believe it or not, did not happen at a Walmart. It was 2008, and I was in a mall in Syracuse, New York. I was in this sports store looking at a signed NFL helmet signed by Dan Marino, which was my favorite dolphin of all time. The price on the helmet was $600. I was telling my young children how that was a lot of money when this guy chimed in about how it might not even be real. He said a lot of these types of memorabilia were forged. I tried to be polite and I said, "Yeah, I guess it is." And I tried to walk away. He followed me through the store and proceeded to tell me that ticket prices were way too high also. Then he asked me, as I was walking away, if I had ever been to a game. I said yes and kept walking. He then decided in his fucked-up brain that he needed to know where I lived and where I was from. I could not get rid of this guy. I had to walk out of the store to get rid of him.

Dentist Trip

I will start this one at the beginning with my tooth. I was on my way to New York for a job I had to do. I was eating a piece of teriyaki jerky and noticed that a piece of my tooth was missing. I was, like, "What the fuck happened to my tooth?" All I could think was that it was going to start aching, and I was going to be on this job for five weeks. It did not start aching while I was on-site, which I was very thankful for.

Then came the day for my appointment to get my tooth fixed at the dentist office. Just like any other dentist appointment, I showed up early on the off chance they could get me in quick. I checked in, and they asked me to review the same form I had reviewed one hundred times before. That really pissed me off, by the way. I then took a seat and waited to be called to the back of the office. There was no one else in the waiting room except for me. Must had been a slow day, I guess. I was sitting there minding my own business when someone else came in. I shot the cursory glance his way just to see who it was. I didn't know him. So he checked in and then decided to sit down right next to me. I mean, in the chair right next to me. I looked around to see if maybe I passed out, and the waiting room filled up. It had not. It was still empty except for my new buddy and me. I had the time, so I counted the number of empty chairs to try and come up with a reason why he would plant his ass right next to me. Fourteen empty chairs and three bench seats that sit three people each. So now I was wondering, *What in the fuck was he thinking?* He saw me counting the chairs, and I thought he maybe got the hint when he got up to move. I was wrong. He got up to go to the bathroom, and when he came out, he sat right fucking next to me even after he looked right at me, and my face was saying, *Sit your ass somewhere else, assface.* So I got up and moved, hoping captain tagalong would not follow me. I thought, *What the fuck?* And I assumed it was over. Oh, hell no, not for me. Some old lady came in smelling like Bengay and ass crack. I bet you would never guess where she planted her wrinkly old ass. Yep, right fucking next to me. I counted the seats again because I could not believe this. Thirteen empty seats and two empty bench seats. WTF! As if that was not enough. She started making this sound like a wild boar in the rain forest. Annoying as all hell. Now, I was irritated enough to pull the wings off a baby bird, and this old whore started reading "Out fucking loud." Just then, they called my name. That probably saved someone's life that day.

I thought, *Thank fucking God. My day of bullshit had to be over.* Not! I needed an X-ray of my tooth, so the assistant leaned me back in the chair just enough to have the lights shining right in my eyes, so I had to squint. She put the god-awful film holder in my mouth. You know, the one that cuts under your tongue and digs into the roof of your mouth. Then she grabbed the lead-filled blanket to drape over me. She swung it in the air to lay it over me, and when it came down, it made direct contact with my balls. Of course, I jumped, and she apologized, as I was cussing. It's funny now, but it wasn't then. Happy fucking Tuesday to me. Now I was numb from my forehead to my neck with spit running down my face and dripping off my chin onto my shirt, and my balls hurt so bad I was sick to my stomach. WTF!

Boo-Hoo Gas

I was getting gas the other day. Just minding my own business and filling up my tank. If you were facing the pumps, I was at one island of pumps on the right side of it. Someone else was on the left side. There were two other islands across from me with people on both sides of each island. There was this old lady in the middle island trying to get gas, I assumed.

I heard this sound, "Boo-hoo, boo-hoo."

I thought nothing of it until I heard it a few more times. I turned my head and looked over to the middle island, and there was this little old black lady dressed like she just left church.

Now she was waving and shouting, "Boo-hoo!"

I walked over to see what she needed. She asked me to fill her car up with gas because she didn't know how. Her husband died five years ago, and he never taught her how to pump gas. She told me that she always came to a crowded gas station so she could have someone else pump her gas. She needed to move to Jersey where they had to pump your gas for you. Yes, I pumped the gas for her. She thanked me and asked me take her money in and pay for it also, and I did. WTF!

Target, Will You Open This

This one happened during the Christmas shopping season, so there were people everywhere. I walked into the Target store to purchase some Christmas gifts for the kids. When I walked in, I saw a lady in a wheelchair by the exit doors. Keep in mind, there were people coming and going in droves. When I walked past her, she was trying to open a bag of candy. I thought nothing of it as I made my way past her to get to the bathroom because I had to take a piss. I went in and took a piss, washed my hands, and dried them. This all took about three to four minutes. I walked out of the bathroom and started to walk by her, and she stopped me and asked me to open a bag of candy for her. Of course, I opened the bag and handed it back to her. I just wondered why she waited to ask me because I saw her struggling with it when I passed her the first time on the way to the bathroom. I guess people just liked talking to me.

Mommy and Sissy Are Coming

I know I have not written in a while, but I have been busy, so get the fuck off my back. This one happened at the Browns Ferry Nuclear Plant Training Center. Let me start this story by laying out the atmosphere at one of these nuclear training facilities. When you were attending one of these computer-based training classes, the rules were very strict to the point of dismissal, if not followed. There was no talking or cell phones, period. There was a proctor in each room to ensure there was no cheating or rules being broken. You started by reviewing the material to be tested on, and when you were ready you raise your hand for what seemed like twenty minutes, and the proctor would come to you to set up the test you were ready to take. After all, the tests were taken you had to sign a roster stating you were there, and you were the one taking the tests. Were you getting the picture? This was serious business.

The proctor for this particular class was about forty years old with red hair, about shoulder length. She was probably about 5 feet, 6 inches tall, and 150 pounds. Kind of homely looking but not hideous. Not that what she looked like mattered but just trying to paint you a picture to make you feel like you were there. I bet you were ready to hear what happened. She waddled up to my desk to put in her password so I could take a test.

And she said in a voice like a five-year-old little girl, "Did I tell you that mommy and sissy are coming to visit?"

I was talking about the whole hand-waving and the voice pitch of a five-year-old. I, of course, said no. You did not tell me because I had never seen you before or talked to you before this very moment. She then proceeded to tell me that she had to vacuum, sweep, mop, pressure wash the deck, do the dishes, laundry, make the beds, wash the windows, and buy groceries. Remember now that it was supposed to be quiet like a library in this room.

Then she said, as I was looking at her in awe because I could not believe I was listening to this shit, "I have to mow the lawn." And this was a two-thousand-square-foot house.

I could not pass that up, so I said, "You have to mow the lawn in your house?"

She looked at me like I was stupid and said, "No, the lawn is outside." Then she asked me if she told me that they were coming from Georgia and Florida. Once again, I said no because I had never talked to you before. You must be a little slow.

Why does this always happen to me? WTF!

No Ice

The family and I pull up to the local Taco Bell because it was our favorite Mexican restaurant. We were going somewhere so we chose to pull through the drive-through. As usual, we pulled up to the speaker, and after a couple rounds of I-don't-know-what-I-want, we finally got our order placed. We pulled up to the window, and I paid the bill because none of these other fuckers were going to pay the bill. The girl handed out our meals and drinks. I said thank you and started handing them to the freeloaders in the back seat (my kids), when I noticed there was no ice in any of the drinks. I leaned out the window and knocked on the little folding window to get her attention. I told her there was no ice in any of the drinks.

She said, "I know, that's because our ice machine is broken."

I could see that there was a Dairy Queen about half a block down the road. So I asked her to stick her head out the window and looked down the street to the Dairy Queen. She looked down the street and saw what I was looking at. I then asked her to take the drinks down to the Dairy Queen to get some ice for the drinks. She looked at me with this blank stare and a look of fear, for some reason, with her mouth agape.

She started to speak and say, "I don't think my boss will let me do that."

I told her I was just joking. Meanwhile, the kids were in the backseat just laughing their asses off. The look on this poor girl's face was priceless.

Hard Hat Names

This is another one about a nuclear plant. The plant is called Browns Ferry and is located in Alabama. Nothing unusual happened this particular day. I just started noticing all the names on the hard hats and decided to write them down. So here were some of the names:

- Fireball
- Ellie May aka "Snap"
- Skillet
- Froggie
- Tadpole (Froggie's son, I asked)
- Kool-Aid
- Both Moon and Sunshine
- Fuzz
- Lardass
- Lizard
- Sweet Rita
- Bam Bam
- Koma Slick

- Nuke 'Em All
- Sting Ray
- The forklift driver they called "Pic"

The funniest thing I saw there was the man they called Tooth. I think they used him for the bubba teeth you get at a novelty store; they must have used him to make the mold. Poor fucker.

Purple Bubble Gum

This one happened a while ago. We used to take two vehicles when we traveled, so we used walkie-talkies instead of cell phones to talk to each other. We were in Charlotte, North Carolina, and as we drove past this little store, we heard this little girl over the radio say to her dad, "Daddy, what are you doing?"

He said, "Buying some cigarettes."

She said, "Daddy, why are you buying cigarettes?"

No answer from Daddy. As you could tell, he was getting frustrated.

Then she said, "Daddy, will you buy me the purple buggle dum?"

He said, "Fine, I will buy you the gum. Now stay off the radio."

She said, "Okay, Daddy." Then a couple of seconds later, she said, "Daddy."

He said, "What!"

She said, "I have to go pottie."

And that was the last thing we heard. We were laughing our asses off by this time.

One Thousand Questions at the Grocery Store

This one happened when we were in the grocery store getting supplies for the place at the lake. We were going through the check-out line, and the cashier asked me what we were doing, and I told her we were going to the lake to go wakeboarding. Here is a list of the questions she asked like we were being interrogated.

- Where are we going?
- Have we been there before?
- Did we like wakeboarding?
- Do all the kids like wakeboarding?
- Do we have our own boat?
- What kind of boat?
- What color is the boat? And on and on and on.

Then the cashier behind me started asking questions. I was, like, "What the fuck and why are these people so interested in what I am doing?" The kids thought I knew these people and asked how I knew them. I assured them I had no idea who they were. Not really funny, but another example of how people just start talking to me like they know me, and I don't know why.

Cat and Dog

This one is not a story of mine but one I heard while up at the lake. This guy started the story with "When I was with my ex-wife, we had a tiny dog. He weighed less than three pounds. We also had a cat, and that fat bitch weighed over twenty-five pounds."

That was how the story started, and I was thinking to myself, *No big deal.* As I had seen little dogs and fat fucking cats. Then he proceeded to tell us that the dog would sit on the arm of the couch and wait for the cat to come strolling by. When the cat reached engagement distance, the dog would jump on the cat's back and wrap his legs around the cat. This, of course, would start the cat up and make her run through the house like she was on fire, up the stairs, down the stairs, into the kitchen, and down the hallway. Then back up the stairs and down the stairs. This would go on until the cat was totally exhausted. As she slowed down and felt all the energy had been drained from her body, the dog would ride her to the floor while the cat lay there, not being able to move. At that point, the dog would let go and start humping the shit out of the cat. When he had completed his dry humping of the cat, the dog would jump back up on the arm of the couch and wait for the cat to regain its strength for another round of ride, and fuck that pussy. I never thought of that approach, just latch on until they were too tired to fight you off. I didn't think women would like that too much, but there were some out there that just wanted to be ridden any way they could.

I Hate Fruit

Here is one that I found very funny but not sure why. Maybe you had to be there, but I am writing about it anyway, so buckle up for boredom. We were at the campground making our normal rounds, on the golf cart, visiting the people we normally associated with during the camping season. We ended up at Ella's camper. She was a very nice and funny lady, kind of short, with gray hair, and no chin whiskers. Her daughter Tracy had a camper right across the little dirt road from Ella. Tracy was, of course, younger and did not have gray hair but did have one chin whisker, which was so long it was all I could see when I looked at her. She was a very nice lady, but that one whisker just fucked me up, and yes, it was coming out of a mole. She had to know I was staring at it every time we talked. I was thinking about it as I was writing this, and I just wanted to reach up, wrap my hand around it, and rip it out. Anyway, we started bullshitting with Ella about normal everyday shit. Out of nowhere, Tracy showed up, and Ella's husband, Butch, came out of the trailer. Then Steve, Butch's brother, showed up with his wife, Diane. Next thing you know, Jennifer showed up, that nosy fucking bitch. She always got her nose in people's business. We started talking about how women pissed their pants when they got older whenever they coughed or sneezed or laughed. We were all laughing, and Ella decided to take Jennifer into the trailer to show her how much a well-placed Bounty paper towel would help with all the pissing. While Jennifer was in the trailer, Tracy and I walked over to her trailer to get a bottle of wine.

We brought it back to Ella's trailer and opened it for consumption. No one else really liked the wine, so I ended up drinking almost the whole bottle by myself. So now the stage was set, and you had an idea of what was happening at this time. We were all just sitting around watching me drink wine and bullshitting about normal everyday shit when the subject of fruit came up.

Tracy said, "I hate fruit."

I said, "What kind of fruit?"

She said, "All fruit." And she went into detailed scenarios about how much she hated fruit. She said, "The other day, I was cutting up some cantaloupe for Donny, her husband, and I was gagging because it smells so bad it is giving me the dry heaves."

It also had all these slimy seeds that she had to clean out of it, and she made a face like she just stepped in fresh dog shit with no shoes on. She said she could not even finish the job of cutting up the cantaloupe until she stuffed pieces of Bounty paper towel into each nostril. At this point, I was laughing my ass off because of the faces she was making. You could tell she really hated fruit. I had never heard anyone talk about fruit like she did. She hated everything about every fruit. She then told us she had a horse that liked apples but had to eat them whole because she couldn't stand to cut into an apple. It made her shiver like running fingernails down a chalkboard. She didn't even like strawberries, WTF. When it came to tomatoes, you can forget it. She said she would rather gut a deer then slice a tomato. I thought it was safe to say that if you invited Tracy over to your place, she would not be bringing a fruit salad, but for some fucked-up reason, she would be bringing that one long hair sticking out of that mole.

Putting the Boat in

This was one of those things that just pissed you off when it happened. It was the middle of the week, and we are at the lake. Not another camper in site. It looked like we were the only people at the lake. I decided to put the boat in so Zaq and I could go fishing. I was going to take it out the same day because I was leaving for a week and didn't want the boat in the water while I was gone. I was assuming it was going to be quick because there was not another soul in sight. As usual, I was wrong. We moseyed on down to the boat ramp, thinking it was going to be quick, and I would be kicked in the nuts if there wasn't someone at the boat ramp putting their boat in the water. I had never seen these people at the campground before today. They took their sweet-ass time putting their boat in the water, and every minute that passed was pissing me off more. I got over it, and it was now our turn to put our boat in the water. We went fishing for about four hours. We had a good time and caught some fish. It was just a nice day. On the way back to the dock, I was thinking to myself how quick it would be to get the boat back on the trailer with no one around. I was wrong again. Could you believe those same mother-fuckers were at the ramp, trying to get their boat out of the water? Fuck me! Story of my life.

Fucked at the Drive-Through

Just thought I would let everyone know that I got fucked at the drive-through once again. I ordered a burger, onion rings, and a Coke. What I received was a burger, 7Up, and french fries. Typical bullshit for a day in my life. WTF?

Six if You Go by Weight

I went to lunch the other day with a couple of guys I worked with. When we walked into this restaurant, the lady at the podium asked how many. There were three of us standing there. Dennis said three, and I cut in and said six, if you went by weight. She sat us at a table for six. We were all old fat fuckers, and that was why I said that. We were having a normal lunch, discussing work and other things. We were just about to finish up, and this old lady walked up to our table and started talking to me like she knew me. She was probably seventy-five years old with gray hair. She started with telling me how she used to work at a drive-in restaurant when she was young. She then told me she was engaged to be married, but her man was off in the war.

I said, "So you were at the drive-in running around on your roller skates and chasing young boys?"

She said, "No, but I did meet one, and I married him, and I am still married to him today." I asked her if she was happy. She said, "Yes, I guess, but if he dies, I am not getting married again unless he has $10,000,000 and no dick."

We laughed, and I could not believe she said that to a complete stranger. The guys I was with asked me how I knew her. I told them I had never seen her before in my life.

Another Walmart Trip

I have not been out a lot lately, so I have not written much. I did go out to the Walmart the other night. What a surprise, right? I went to buy some Christmas presents for the kids. We bought one of the boys the new Madden NFL game. No big deal until we got to the counter to pay and the cashier was like a chatty Kathy Doll with Downs syndrome and a fifty-inch string that had been pulled to the very end. She started with asking who the game was for. I told her my two sons would be playing the game. She proceeded to tell me the game had too many buttons to push, but she would recommend a game that she did not know the name of. She continued on with "If you beat the first Greek god, then you have to beat the next one. It is kind of bloody and messy, so I would not recommend it for your eleven-year-old." And on and on she went. It might not have been so bad if her eyes were not so far apart. WTF?

More Nicknames from Hard Hats

- Bucket head
- CoCo

- Tennis shoes
- Bones
- My Brutha
- Fathead
- Munch

CVS Pharmacy

This one is not that funny, but it has never happened to me, so I thought I would write it down. Zaq had a basketball game the other night, so we all loaded up to go watch him play. We left a little early, so we could stop by the CVS pharmacy to pick up some prescriptions. I pulled up to the window, and it was open. They made eye contact with me, but as usual, they just ignored you until you pushed the buzzer. I guess they figured we were not ready to order just yet, like there was a menu or something. There was usually this crusty old bitch that was working there, but she was not on duty. I was relieved to learn that information. Maybe her broom could not make it through all the snow. Anyhow, I finally pushed the call button to get their attention, and this nasty young bitch came over to help us. She was throwing the pills around and even tossed the clipboard across the table. I could tell she was in a pissy mood. She finally handed me the pills and said, "Have a nice night."

I said, "Have a nice night yourself."

She answered me with "I will most certainly not have a nice night." And she slammed the window closed. What a bitch.

Sam's Club

I was in Sam's Club the other day to pick up a few things. I was walking around, and the urge to take a piss hit me hard. I started making my way back to the bathrooms, and an old guy in one of the motorized carts was blocking the way. It seemed as though he ran into the pop machine and could not figure out how to back up the cart. So I asked if he needed help, and he grunted and told me to mind my own business, so I did. I managed to squeeze by him and make my way into the bathroom. Just as I got my zipper down and my dick out to piss, here came Dale Earnhardt into the bathroom. He ducked into one of the stalls very quickly and managed not to close the door. Just as my stream started to flow, I looked up and in the mirror. All I saw was an old ass and balls with a diaper pulled halfway down his legs to the knees. Lucky for me, I got to see the sight just as he bent over to lower the seat. I wish he would have lowered the seat first, but that was not how my life went. So I pulled my eyes away from the mirror and continued with my piss. Apparently, he got turned around and managed to plant his ass on the seat. Just as I was shaking off my serpent, I heard this loud fart and a whew from the patron inside. It sounded like he blew the back off the toilet, and what followed, I could not even describe. I quickly zipped up, washed my hands, and left.

What a Day

Let me tell you how my last Saturday went. First of all, Marysa was trying to get ready for a night out on the town, but the plug-in in her bathroom was not working. I figured, no problem. I would run downstairs and flip the breaker because it was probably tripped. The breaker would not reset. Every time I reset it, it snapped back with authority like it was saying, "Fuck you, Mike." I was thinking, *Shit, now I have to replace the breaker.* I figured this was no problem. While the power was off, I would replace the breaker and a couple of outlets that were worn-out. So off to the Home Depot I went to pick up the items I needed to perform the task at hand. Luckily, I brought the old breaker to make sure I got the right one and not have to make two trips because that really pissed me off. Because it was a ground fault breaker, it costs sixty-five dollars instead of eight dollars. That pissed me off, but you couldn't take shortcuts, so I grabbed the breaker, and off to the checkout I went. So far so good. I got home and headed to the basement to pop in the new breaker. I shut off the power to the box this time, as I thought that might be a wise move. After some coaching from my brother Doug, I connected the ground wire and the other wires to the breaker and flipped the main power back on. I flipped the new breaker to the on position, and again, it said, "Fuck you, Mike." And it flipped back. Now I was thinking it was something serious and halfway expected it because that was how my life went. I called Doug back, and he told me to take apart the receptacles to see if any of the wires were exposed and grounding out the breaker. Of course, I found nothing wrong, and in the process of doing this, in the fucking dark, I broke the plug-ins in the kid's bathroom. At this point, I figured I was going to have to call an electrician and got the whole house rewired. While the power was out, I decided to replace the two outlets I had planned on replacing anyway. In the process of replacing the outlets, I heard water dripping. I thought maybe it was the snow melting off the roof. It was not snow melting. With the power off to the pump to the fish tank upstairs, it started leaking all over the floor and down into the basement. Now I had water all over the floor on two levels of the house. Fuck me! I started cleaning up the water and stopped the leak, so I thought I had to take the pump apart and grease up the O-rings. Somehow shrimp got into the pump, and when I took the pump apart, they started jumping around in the sink. To recap, there was no power to the house, breakers still didn't work, the fish tank was draining into the house, wires were sticking out of the wall, and wet clothes were in the dryer while I was trying to catch shrimp in the dark so I could get them back in the tank before they would die. Fuck! I got the water cleaned up and the shrimp back in the tank. Now back to the breakers and the outlets. New outlets were in, and the power was back on. The breaker was still not working, but I would deal with that later. I grabbed the vacuum to clean up my mess. I turned on the vacuum, and the fucking belt broke (son of a bitch). Was this day ever going to end? Luckily, I had a spare belt, so I changed that and cleaned up the mess. At this point, I was thinking that must be the end of my shitty day. I made myself some mozzarella sticks and some ranch dip with sour cream and a glass of ice water. I sat down in the blue dueling recliners. I hate those fucking things because it was so hard to get the footrest down once it was up. Shit, I forgot a napkin, so I leaned forward and kicked hard to get the footrest down (no joy). Both recliners tipped forward, and I lost the plate and the water. The plate broke and so did the water glass when they hit the floor. Now there was glass everywhere. The answer to my question of would this shitty day ever end had now been answered. Marysa called and I started telling her how my day was going (looking for some sympathy). All she was doing was laughing, and as the story went on, she laughed harder. What a fucking day. I got an electrician coming next week to look at the wiring in the house. Two days later, as I was pulling into the driveway, I noticed the extension cord plugged into the golf cart was not working. I knew this because it was one of the cords that had a light at the end, so you knew if it was working. I guess it was to be expected because it was lying in about three inches of water in the carport. I unplugged the cord and hung it up to dry. I was thinking to myself that the outlet the cord was plugged into was controlled by the breaker that kept tripping. Then I was thinking that there was no way it could be that easy because nothing was ever that easy for me. So I bebopped down to the basement and flipped the breaker to on, and it actually stayed the fuck on. That was easy. Fuck me! Story of my life.

Stewed Tomatoes

When I was a young child, I went to live with my aunt for a while because my parents were splitting up. I was young enough that I didn't mind because there were lots of other kids there. I think my aunt had nine or ten kids or her own that lived. She even took in foster kids on top of that. You would think that with that many kids around, you could get away with some wrongdoings. That would be a wrong assumption. This lady had game, and you were not going to get anything by her, and if she told you not to do something, like crawl up on the garage roof, you better not do it. There were no time-outs or counting to three. It was directly to the wooden spoon in half a second, and that ass was getting beat. I would tell you that she never whipped me when I didn't deserve it. I deserved every beating I got, and I thank her for it. The things I hated the most about living there was church all the fucking time. Five days a week, we went church, church, and more fucking church. The stewed tomatoes and hominy were gross. I didn't like tomatoes, but stewed tomatoes were like eating a wet fur ball dipped in panther piss. I would rather have my balls pounded flat with a rawhide mallet than eat stewed tomatoes. I would sit at the table for hours with my arms crossed and lips pursed until she would let me get up from the table. Don't let me forget the fucking powdered milk. Not a stewed tomato, but running a close second to it. Like drinking diarrhea strained through a basketball net. Warm, chunky nasty shit and the god-awful smell— it smelled like a cross between dirty clothes hamper, crotch from a whore's pantyhose, and ball sweat. I hate milk to this day.

Family from Across the Street

Let me try to paint you a picture of the family that lived across the street from where I grew up. The family crest would be known as the Neff Family. Let me start with the Dad. His name is Andy. Let me take you back to the time when I was growing up. I think every neighborhood or at least every town had that one family with one of the members missing an eye, a finger, a toe, or a seventeen-year-old kid who still had a baby arm on his left side. I think you get the point that by luck of the draw, someone was going to be fucked up. Andy had one good eye, and the other was always kind of cloudy and a little Pusey. He was a boss out at the local chemical plant. He was maybe 5 feet, 8 inches and weighed about 160 pounds, I am guessing. Donna, the mom, worked at a restaurant as a cook. I think she weighed in at about 320 pounds and had blackheads the size of an eraser on a yellow number 2 pencil. As a kid, looking at that was just nasty. Nice lady but dirty. Danny, the oldest boy, believe it or not, was also short one optic. Got his taken out with a golf club. That had to hurt. If you are keeping track, then you should know that we are up to two people in the same family that are visually challenged. Their bulldog

Ralph was also visually impaired with one good eye and one that was just cloudy and dripping with puss all the time. I'm telling you I did not want to go over there without a full-faced motorcycle helmet on or at least a face shield and a pair of safety glasses. Danny tipped the scales at about 250 pounds in those days and got bigger as time went on, just like the rest of us. He ended up in a wheelchair with MS and died way too young. That is very sad because he was a really nice guy.

Next is Kevin. He was the redheaded retarded kid in the family. Always nice but kind of out there. And he was not really retarded, like with Down syndrome, but he was out there. I think he joined the army and never saw him since. Next came Robbie, who is kind of taller and thinner than the rest of the family and never had a girlfriend. Didn't think much about that then, but when he got older and moved to Seattle to become a turd burglar, it all made sense. Last I heard, he was still there puffing peter. Not that there is anything wrong with that. I have nothing against homos. I believe they were made that way, and there is nothing they can do about it.

Next comes the girls. Kathy is kind of a chunky, reddish blond-haired girl that you knew was going to end up looking like her mother. Don't know what happened to her, but if I find out, I will add that later to the book. Maybe a Neff chapter 2? Next comes Chrissy, a skinny little girl and kind of cute when she was young. She turned out to be a thieving crackhead, is what I hear, which is not hard to believe if you stay in Butte without an education. The last one is Sissy, and I have no idea what happened to her. I also think there were a couple of them who didn't make it past the birth canal.

You may think I was little harsh on this family, but I was trying to get you to see who they are so you will understand the rest of the story, and it kind of gives you a visual of them. Now from memory, I will try to describe what the neighborhood called the Neff House. The bedrooms had bare walls and unfinished sheetrock with holes here and there. Clothes, blankets, and garbage everywhere, and in most rooms, you could not see the floor. The hallways had holes in the walls, with dirt and shit everywhere. The bathroom smelled like a carnival porta potty on its last day in town. The bathtub was always full of clothes. You could ask me why it was full of clothes, and my answer would be "I have no fucking clue." Maybe because there was no more room on the floor in their bedrooms. The sink and counter looked like the bathroom at truck stop or biker bar.

The next stop on the tour of the Neff abode was the lovely dining facility. Oh my fucking god! This place was teeming with microorganisms never seen before by man, scientist, or animal. The table and counters were always covered with food and dirty dishes, sometimes weeks old. There would be open jars of peanut butter and mayonnaise on the counter. Maybe even a half-eaten sandwich or two just sitting there and molding. And the smell, oh my god the smell, was like a cross between a dirty clothes hamper and a skunk's cunt. Let's just say when you walked in, you felt physically assaulted and not in the good way. You couldn't tell if the stench was coming from the sink, table, open jar of mayonnaise, or the garbage can you could not see. I was not sure if there was an actual garbage can. I did not physically see the can but assumed it was there because that was where the rotting garbage was piled the highest. Anyway, the smell from the bathroom that was right off the kitchen and the smell from the kitchen combined would bring a tear to a pig farmer's eye.

Next stop on the tour is the living room. I am not sure how anything but bacteria could have lived in there, but somehow, the family thrived. The carpet is hard to describe other than fucking nasty. Not sure what color the carpet started out as, but in my memory, it was shit brown with burn holes, crusty matted-down oil and dirt stains, mayo, peanut butter spots, and let's not forget the dog and cat shit. Not sure if they owned a vacuum, but if they did, it was probably under all the clothes that were piled up in the bathtub. The couch and chairs just blended with the carpet with all the same stains and burn holes, and of course, everyone had half-eaten bowls of cereal tucked neatly under the couch and on the floor just below that half-eaten sandwich that was tucked underneath the couch cushion. Hopefully, by now you have a visual of the inside of this house.

The outside did not look any better. The walls on the outside were tar paper, siding, plywood, or a combination of all three, depending on what wall you were looking at. The yard had no grass, so when it rained, it turned into a mud hole, so it was a good thing they took their shoes off at the door. That was a joke; you know where all that mud went, don't you! Yep, right in the house. Don't even think about the garage. Even the American Pickers would not attempt to go in there.

Now that you have a picture of the family and the house, I will tell you a couple of stories that happened in the neighborhood. We would fuck with these guys all the time. I should mention before you get butt hurt that they were our friends, and we were not bullying them. Most of the time, they were in on the shit with us. One year after Christmas, my mom took the tree down and asked me to take it into the alley and put it with the trash. I told my mom no problem. On my way to the alley with the tree I had, what I thought was a better idea with the tree turned out not a better idea. My thought was to take the tree over to Neff Manor and knock on the door, and when they opened the door, we would run the tree into the living room and run like hell. I was thinking this would be a win-win. The house would get a much-needed air freshener, and it would be funny. I was thinking fun would be had by all. This was not the case, and because Andy was in the living room at the time and we hit him with the tree, he did not find it amusing at all. My parents also did not find it amusing, and I knew that by the pain my ass was feeling from my dad's leather belt being up close and personal. I think my mom might have laughed a little bit, but she wouldn't let me see that.

Another time I took two small branches that, when put together, barely covered my face. I had what I thought was another good idea, as I was full of good ideas that summer. One night after it got good and dark, I walked right up to the living room window with the branches covering my face. I thought it was one of the kids sitting there near the window, and I was just going to scare them. I got as close as I could to the window, and as I was pulling one of the branches to the side to make it look like I was looking through a bush, I noticed it was the lord of the manor, Andy. I did get the effect I was looking for because as my full face appeared from behind the bush, it startled the shit out of him because his face was only about a foot from the window. Without the glass there, I was close enough to kiss him. I laughed and ran. He did not laugh and neither did my parents, and again, my ass was introduced to my dad's leather belt. After seeing the look on Andy's face, it was so worth the beating.

Another sunny summer afternoon, we were milling about and a little bored. We decide to head on over to the Neff estate to see if we could muster up another reason for a good beating. As we are parading through the yard, we heard a noise in one of the bedrooms, so we got a bucket so we could look in the window. We couldn't believe it. There was the prince of the Neff castle thumbing through a *Hustler* magazine and trying like hell to pull the skin off his dick or so it seemed because he was really going to town. I knocked on the window and yelled, "You are going to kill that thing if you keep beating it like that." We took off running, and I assumed I was in for another beating. He never said anything to my parents, so I dodged that beating. Not that it mattered because that was a summer full of beatings for me. I think I got about four or five every week that summer. I will say I never got one I didn't deserve.

Personal GI Joe

Let me tell you a story about my two older brothers and how they treated me like their personal life-size GI Joe. I am five years younger than them, just to let you know. We lived two blocks away from an overpass that stretched over the interstate that ran through the middle of town. It is important to understand that this overpass played a huge role in our childhood. Let me explain. It was the boundary between neighborhoods (us and them). Not a different class, just a boundary, and they went to different grade schools than we did. It was our sledding hill in the winter. It was where we floated our inner tubes to in the summer because it also stretched over the creek that ran through town. It was the boundary in that direction we could not pass when we were really young, maybe four or five years old. It was where we rode our skateboards with no pads or helmets because we weren't pussies, and you would have gotten your ass kicked for wearing them in that town unless you were special maybe. It was where we launched different shit off the top onto traffic going down the interstate. That was very stupid and got my ass beaten for that. It was probably a good thing my dad did not have his name on his belt because it would have probably been permanently carved into my ass cheeks. It was the landmark that let you know you were close to home and back in your neighborhood where it was safe. No other kids would follow you over the bridge into our neighborhood for fear of getting a sound thrashing. Our neighborhood had, what you might call, a bad reputation or at least a rough and tough reputation. It was also the overpass that had stairs running down the side with metal handrails. Maybe wide enough for one person to navigate either up or down. This was where it got all fucked up and my brothers turn into giant dickheads. I was maybe six or seven years old, and my loving brothers thought it would be good idea to put me on one of those metal saucers and see if I could make it to the bottom of the stairs. The stairs were full of snow and ice. It was probably about negative ten degrees, so colder that Frosty's nut sack. Of course, I didn't want to do it because I saw the potential hazards of breaking something, but they didn't care because I was their personal GI Joe. So onto the saucer they planted me and got me to the edge of the stairs. I was sure I was calling them names as they gave me a big push, and down the icy stairs I went like a rocket. I made it about halfway before my knee caught a handrail, and it was all a hellish blur from there. I made it to the bottom but not before my knee, elbow on one arm, and my wrist on the other arm were fucked up. I also hit my head a couple of times. They laughed, called me a pussy, and told me to walk it off. I cried and limped home, not knowing what part of my body to hold because it hurt everywhere, to tell my mom what those motherfuckers did to me.

On a different day, on the other side of the overpass was a huge culvert that the creek ran through. Of course, it was January, so it was cold as fuck. Just like any little kid, I wanted so badly to hang out with my older brothers. I didn't know why because they were fucking mean to me. So they devised a scheme to allow me to hang out with them. I had to go through an initiation. I just knew this would be fucked up, and the potential for bodily energy would be at an all-time high. Their idea was for me to get on an inner tube at the top of the overpass and ride it off the top of the culvert into the creek below. Let's not forget it was January in Montana, and the only reason the creek wasn't froze over solid was because it was moving pretty fast right there. So they got me on the tube at the top of the hill and pointed me at the creek. With a nice hard push and a fuck you, down the hill I went. Their aim was perfect because I went right off the top center of the culvert and right into the middle of the creek. Son of bitch, that water was cold! I could still feel it as I am writing this now. This was the seventies, so of course, I was wearing bell-bottom jeans. As I got out of the water, they started to freeze almost instantly. By the time I got back to the top of the hill to head home, they were frozen solid, and it looked I was ringing a bell with every step I took. My older brothers and friends were laughing their asses off, fucking assholes. I could have died of hypothermia if I didn't live so close. My mom was pissed, to say the least.

For some reason, when we were really young, my mother thought it was a good idea for us all to take a bath together. I know now it was probably to make it easier on her. We never gave it any thought, and I surely never thought I would be in any danger, especially from another family member. Just the fact that I mentioned danger should let you know one of those dickheads was about to torture me in some way. As the tub was filling and we were all sitting there, butt-ass naked (me with the biggest dick, of course), for some reason, my oldest brother Doug decided to reach up and turn off the cold water. I thought maybe he did that because he just came in from playing tackle football out in the street. This was in February, so it was cold, and the streets were covered with snow. The hot water was still flowing, and he decided to put my head under the scolding water. I was screaming bloody murder as my mom came in to see what the hell was going on. She caught the fucker red-handed, and he knew his number was up. As it was back then, it was an eye for an eye, and in true fashion and believing that 100 percent, she grabbed him and stuck his head under the hot water. Later, I found out why he did it. He is five years older than me, but when he saw my dick in the tub, he got insanely jealous.

The credit for the next one goes to my brother Greg, who is the one, I believe, who made me afraid of heights. In the seventies in Butte, Montana, we had privately owned department stores because the unions would not let the big chain stores in without paying huge wages, so they stayed away. This particular day, we were at the Hennessey building in uptown Butte. I believe it was six or seven stories high. We were on one of the top floors when my mom herded us boys up to leave. As we started down the marble stairs with the metal edging, I spotted a dime on one of the top steps. As I bent over to pick up the dime, my brother Greg decided at that very moment it would be a good idea to give me a push. That push sent me flying down the stairs all the way to the bottom. It is a wonder I am alive today, having the brothers I did growing up. I did not break anything that day, but I had been nervous around high places ever since that day. Thanks, dickhead.

Little Richard

This is in reference to a third cousin twice removed or some shit like that we called Little Richard. Not really sure how we were related. I am not really sure I give a shit. I was more worried about sports and, of course, what my next mission would be as my brothers' personal life-size GI fucking Joe or when the next fight would be. Anyway, here we go. I will describe the family and then get to the story.

Little Richard was the dad of this family and weighed in about four hundred pounds. If not four hundred pounds, he couldn't be more than a wheat thin shy of that. He was roughly five feet, ten inches tall and a nice guy really. I am not sure if he bathed, but he smelled like a dirty clothes hamper and ball sweat mixed together. It was a rancid smell that if you got close enough, it made you feel dirty. His wife was Kathy, I think her name was, but I am not sure. She tipped the scales at about 275 pounds, I believe. Probably about five feet, one inch tall. The smell was like the crotch of a set of dirty nylons and blue cheese dressing mixed together. It was not pleasant to say the least. I also remember a couple of kids that also had outstanding potential to reach maximum density. They were all very nice people, but as a kid, different things stick in your mind. That is how I remember them, whether it is right or wrong. I remember them driving an old, faded blue station wagon that the shocks were completely trashed on. The windows were so dirty you could not see in them. It was like a natural tent and was not only on the outside. The windshield was so dirty I can't believe they didn't get in a wreck. You could not see one square inch of the floor. It was like someone dumped four large garbage cans of trash in the car. It smelled like the city dump. You couldn't see the dashboard, and I am sure shit fell off the dash every time they hit a bump or took a turn. So they would show up every summer, and my mom would welcome them with open arms like any good Christian would do. She would always fix them something to eat, and boy could they eat. They would pound down two loaves of bread worth of sandwiches, a couple gallons of milk, and a couple family-sized bags of chips. When they were done with that, they would each eat an entire row of Oreo cookies. That was just the four of them, but my mom was happy to do it. They were like eating machines. They kind of reminded me of that Hungry Hungry Hippo game. I was little, so I did not want to get in between their mouth and their food. I was scared I would be mistaken for a chicken wing or a piece of licorice. Most of the time we would split when we saw them coming and Mom was home. Of course, we would avoid Mom at all costs because if she saw us, she would make us stay and visit with them. That smell haunts my memories to this day, and I hated being within a mile of them. My mom told me how wrong I was for feeling that way, but the fucking smell was just fucking nasty. Like I said, they were very nice people, but they could have at least hosed each other off if they didn't want to bathe. Maybe just a little something to knock the crust off. Maybe a change of clothes or a trip through the sprinkler might help. I remember, if we knew Mom was not home and we spotted them pulling into town, it didn't matter if we were blocks from the house or miles. We would take off on our bikes like a bat out of hell, pedaling as fast as we possibly could. We had to beat them to the house to close it up to make it look like we were not home. We took every possible shortcut through alleys, yards, and vacant lots pedaling until our legs were burning. The mad dash to the house always ended in our alley by jumping off the still-moving bikes and making a mad dash through the passageway between the house and garage onto the closed-in porch. We would dive into the livening room to close the drapes and shut off all the lights in hopes that we beat that big, faded blue, and absolutely filthy chariot to the house before they saw the drapes open. For some reason, back then, if the drapes were closed, it meant don't bother knocking. Now you might say that was not very fucking Christian-like, but you know, kids are evil, and they did smell like a skunk's taint, and it was awful. We went to their house one time, and oh my fucking god, their immune system must be off the charts to be able to live in that squalor.

Just Tell Me

This one took place at a bar in Georgia. There were four of us in a bar getting drunk. It all started when the waitress came over to take our drink order for the sixth time. I looked at her and asked her if she knew she looked like Sandra Bernhard. She could have been her twin. Sarcastically, she said no, never heard that one before. I had a reason I asked her that, so I kept digging. At this point, I should tell you we all had a pretty good buzz going.

I said to her, "I was just wondering if people that look the same have the same desires."

She said, "I don't know." And she left to get our drinks we ordered. When she got back, I asked if she knew about Sandra. She said, "No, why do you ask?"

And I knew; then she took the bait. Since she took the bait, it was time for the next step of my plan. It was still a little iffy, if my assumptions were right, but I asked anyway. I told her that Sandra was bisexual, and I was wondering if she was also. She said no and left the table rather abruptly. One of the guys we were with was all pissed off and told me to stop questioning her like that. I told him to lick my balls and that I was just having fun. If I thought I was really pissing her off, I would have stopped, but something told me she wanted to tell us about her experience with another woman.

The other guys asked, "What the fuck are you doing?"

She would never admit that to us. I told them I was going to get her to tell us about the time she was with a girl if they didn't fuck it up. When she got back to the table again, I told her, "I know you want to tell us, so you might as well get it off your chest." I also told her that she would never see us again because none of us were from that area, and she would feel a lot better not keeping it bottled up.

She looked at me and paused for a second and said, "No, I haven't."

I knew I was right, and I had her. She left the table to get us more drinks. "She is going to tell us," I told the guys, and they still didn't believe it. When she got back with yet another round of drinks (we were getting pretty drunk at this point). I asked her what time she got off.

She told us, "In about an hour."

I asked her if she wanted to join us for some drinks when she got off. To the other guy's disbelief, she said yes. She finished her shift and joined us for some drinks. After a couple of drinks, some jokes, and a bunch of laughter, she started to loosen up and feel comfortable. So I went in for the kill shot and asked her if she would like to share with us her experience she had with another woman. I also told her not to leave out any details. She told us, in detail, about how it was a friend in college who was gay. She got her drunk and seduced her. She also told us that most women in college have at least one homosexual experience in college. She told us she was not gay and had not done anything like that since. I asked her if she felt better now that she has actually told someone. She said she did and thanked me for pushing her.

I told her, "You are welcome." I was really drunk by this time, and I asked her if she wanted to share her stories about the threesomes she had been in and her first anal experience. She declined my offer about the anal but did share her threesome story with us. She had a couple more drinks and left. The guys said they could not believe that I got her to tell us those stories. It was great entertainment, and we may have helped someone that night.

Shitty Liar

We had kind of a crazy morning with Zaq. I think the lie he told me this morning was probably the worst lie I had ever heard or at least one of the worst. We were getting ready to leave to take Zaq to the bus stop, which was not in front of our house for him anymore. That was because he had to go to a school for delinquents, so the bus stop was about a mile from the house, and the school was in a different town not too far away. We were getting ready to leave, so I walked into his bedroom to see if he was ready to go. He had his back to me, and I saw him shove something into his pocket. I asked him what he just shoved in his pocket, and when he turned around, he looked like he just got caught with his hand in the cookie jar. He told me he did not put anything in his pocket, and I said to him, "You are lying." Then he pulled a yellow highlighter out of his pocket. It was just a normal highlighter, but he looked so fucking guilty. I asked him why he looked so guilty and why he was taking the highlighter to school. I had my suspicions, but I wanted to hear his explanation. He said it was to keep food in. I replied with "What the fuck are you talking about?" Now I knew he was up to something. He said, like food, milk, or mashed potatoes. I told him he was lying and that I wanted the truth. We arrived at the parking lot where the bus picked up all the delinquents, and I gave him one more chance to tell me the truth. Then he told me it was to put food in to throw away because he did not want his food touching. I asked him if that was fucking English because that made no sense. I said, "So let me get this straight. You want to take a highlighter to school so you can take it apart, take food off your tray to stuff in the highlighters so you can throw it away without touching. I call bullshit. Now tell me what the truth is."

Well, the bus came, and I told him he better have the truth for me when I picked him up after school. He texted me from the bus and told me some kid at school asked him to bring the highlighter to school. I am sure that was a little closer to the truth but still a lie. He got that lying from his fucked-up piece of shit mother. Turns out it was to put weed in. If you can possibly do it, you need to homeschool your kids.

Crossbow Challenge

This one happened when I was in Kansas visiting my brother Doug. We went out to the farm that was owned by July's family. Not really much out there, as I remember. I saw a rundown house and a barn. There were a couple of old cars and a big farm truck with old, faded green paint and rotting wood side boards. You could see forever because the land was so flat. This was a blistering hot day, not a cloud in the sky, and it was crystal clear without so much as a haze in the air. So we were at Doug's house when we decided to go out to the farm and shoot his crossbow. This was a nice crossbow, not one that you would buy at Walmart. It was used for hunting. My point here is that it was a very powerful crossbow and not some cheap piece of shit toy. We were at the farm shooting the crossbow and having a good time. I could not believe how accurate and powerful it was. I decided I wanted to know just how far this bow would shoot an arrow. I came up with a very stupid idea. I thought I would shoot it straight up in the air to see just how far it would go. Not a good idea and one of the most stupid ideas I had ever had. Doug advised against it, but I was determined to see how far this bow would shoot an arrow. I shot the bow straight up and watched the arrow disappear. The decision we had to make in a split second was which way was the right direction to move so that the arrow did not come down straight through the top of our heads and out our assholes. We decided to make a run for the faded green truck. Guess I forgot about Newton's law of gravity (what goes up must come down). I am pretty sure Doug was a lot more scared than I was, and that split second, I thought, *Care to go for a sleigh ride, motherfucker.*

Kansas Tried to Fuck Me

This was how the State of Kansas, out of the blue, decided I owed them $5,000. I was trying to get a loan for a house, and this lien showed up on my credit report from the State of Kansas. The credit report was showing that I owed the State of Kansas back taxes. I was, like, "WTF, I have never worked in Kansas." I picked up the phone and called the tax office in Kansas to get this cleared up, and they were real assholes to me. I told them I had never worked in the State of Kansas, so I didn't owe them any money. Essentially, they told me to prove it. I asked the crusty old bitch on the phone if I was supposed to get a note from every single employer in the State of Kansas stating that I did not work for any of them.

She said, "I don't know."

And I said, "Then who the fuck knows? Do you people just pull a name out of a hat and decide to fuck them over?"

She said, "We would not do that."

I asked her how in the hell did she get my name then? Of course, she didn't know, and I could tell she didn't give a shit either. I told her I paid taxes in Montana, where I lived, and she said, "Prove it."

I told her I could send her my tax returns, and she said that was not good enough. She would need a letter from the State of Montana on their letterhead. I asked her why she couldn't just call the tax office in Montana, since they were all in the same business of ass raping the public and not even having the common courtesy to give us a reach around, and ask them if I had been paying taxes in Montana. Our fucking government has ruined our country. She said it was not her responsibility to call and clear it up. I asked her if it was her responsibility to pull my name out of a hat and charge me $5,000 dollars. She told me she did not appreciate my language.

I told her, "Whatever, bitch. I don't like getting screwed out of $5,000." I got the letter from the state and sent it to the Kansas office. They accepted it and said I didn't owe them any money at this time. I said that was good, now please take it off my credit report.

"Oh, we don't do that, sir."

I said, "Why the fuck not? You put it on my report, now take it off."

She said, "Someone does that once a month, and it costs twenty-five dollars to make it happen." Or I could wait the seven years until it just went away.

I said, "So let me get this straight: you fucked up my credit due to no fault of mine, you made me spend time getting it cleared up even though you were in the wrong, and now you want me to pay you for the fucking you gave me." My hands were tied, so I sent the bitch the money. They cashed the check, and it was still on my credit report six years later. What a fucking cunt.

Jokesters

Here's one about two guys I was in the Navy with. We didn't join the Navy together, but we were on the same boat at the same time, just to be clear. We were stationed at a base in Little Creek, Virginia. On a ship called the USS *Hermitage* LSD 34. The LSD is an abbreviation for Landing Ship Dock. It was like a dry dock for boats with a front on it so we could cross the ocean. So we would lower our stern gate and basically sink the ship just enough to let smaller boats drive in. Then we would pump the water out, close the gate, and be on our way. As hull technicians, we took care of all that. We also did all the welding, pipefitting, carpentry work, damage control, firefighting, flight operations, and plumbing. I explained all, that so you would understand the type of people I am talking about. There were these two specific guys who were always fucking with each other. One day, John took a shop rag to the head with him and wiped his ass with it when he was done shitting. He told me what he was doing, so I was waiting with great anticipation. He came back to the shop and played it off really well. He started working on a valve he had been working on earlier. He had a can of grease and some oil set out on the table by where he was working. Cliff, the guy who would be the victim of this vicious crime, was working across the table from John, so the set up was perfect. John was using rags to wipe up the oil and grease from this valve and at one point asked Cliff to throw him a rag. Cliff obliged and threw John the rag he asked for. John caught the rag, and without Cliff knowing it, John switched that rag with the one he wiped his ass with. John walked around the table to the side Cliff was on and held the rag up to Cliff's nose and asked him if it smelled like oil. Cliff took a big ole whiff of the rag, and it only took him a second to realize he smelled shit and not oil. He took after John to kill him while I was laughing my ass off.

Raviolis

This one also took place on the USS *Hermitage*. As hull technicians, we do work and favors for every department on the ship. In turn, we got some special privileges because of the work we did for them. If you worked your connections right, you could get anything you wanted anytime you wanted it. That meant you could get food for that late-night snack for when you returned to the ship after getting all fucked up like a soup sandwich. This particular time, we were in Palma de Mallorca, Spain. At about 1700, I went to the mess decks to talk to one of my buddies about getting some food for when we got back from liberty that night. He gave me a gallon can of raviolis for our late-night drunk snacking. We did not have a microwave on the boat, but we did have a rod oven for welding rod. I think it kept the welding rod at about 160 degrees because you could not have any moisture in the flux around the welding rod or they would be no good. So we cleaned out enough of the welding rod to fit the gallon-sized can of ravs in the rod oven. We went out drinking and got completely torn out of the box. One of those nights where we were drinking hard and didn't eat anything after our 1700 meal on the mess decks on the ship. It was about 0100, so we started back to the ship. We were looking for something to eat all the way back, and we could not find a single fucking thing open. We were almost back to the ship, and it hit me; we had raviolis in the rod oven. I told the guys we had the ravs, and everyone high-fived and got excited. As we were boarding the ship, the spirits were high because we were drunk and hungry, but we had line of sight on some food to fill our alcohol-soaked bellies. We headed directly to the shop to partake in our after-hours culinary delight. I pulled the raviolis out of the rod oven. My mouth was watering because I was so hungry. The ends of the can were swollen and rounded to the point that the can would almost not stand up on its own. Being so drunk, we did not pay any attention to the pressure that the can was under. You would think that being in the military, we would have some type of utensil to open up a can of any kind. We could find nothing, so I grabbed a screwdriver. I raised it high in the air and came down with enough force to open the can but not enough for the screwdriver to stay in the can. It opened a hole just big enough to let the sauce out at a one thousand miles per hour. Because the can was rounded on the ends, it tipped over and started spinning like a top. That motherfucker was spinning so fast we couldn't catch it, and it was spewing boiling hot sauce all over all of us. Of course, we were standing in a circle around the can waiting in anticipation of that first bite. That was a bad idea because it splattered each and every one of us. When the can stopped spinning, which seemed like twenty minutes but was probably more like five seconds, we looked at each other and started laughing like a bunch of little school girls. We were so drunk we just stood there and watched this can spin out of control, spewing lavalike sauce all over us. The red sauce was all over our clothes, our faces, our hair, and the shop. Not one of my better ideas.

Mosquitos

This one is about a float trip in Montana on the Big Hole River, I believe it was. The characters on this trip, or should I say nightmare, were my brother Doug; his oldest son, Ben; Jim Colley; Paul Weeks; and me. We all got together and made a plan to float the river. We thought it was a good idea, and we were excited for that day to arrive. We looked at a map and decided where we would put the raft in and where we would take the raft out of the water and get picked up by our wives. We figured the trip would take about two

145

hours, and boy were we wrong. Since we believed it would only take a couple of hours, we did not bring any food or drinks because we were going to all go grab something to eat with the wives at the end of this quick float trip. We figured we could all go two hours without any sustenance.

The big day arrived, and we were at the water's edge with the raft and fishing gear. We kissed and hugged the wives good bye and piled into the raft. It was all going good and a nice easy float, with the water pushing us along at a pretty good pace. Nice scenery everywhere, birds all around, and deer on the banks and even catching a few fish. It was shaping up to be an awesome day. That was when Ben decided to sit up on the edge of the raft and Doug told him not to because there were some rapids coming up. Ben decided he knew more than his dad, so he sat up on the edge anyway. We hit the rapids, and Ben hit the water. Doug was ready for it, so as soon as Ben hit the water, Doug reached in and grabbed him by the hair and pulled him out of the water so we didn't lose him for good. The look of fear on Ben's face was priceless, and his eyes were open wider than silver dollars. He listened to Doug for the rest of the trip. For the first half an hour or so, the trip went well, and we even almost got rid of one mouth to feed, but Doug fucked that up by saving Ben.

Then all of a sudden, the water became almost still, and we were barely moving. The water got really shallow, and the river widened. We were in the middle of a ranch, and the cattle were lined up at the banks of the river partaking in some cool refreshing liquids. It got really hot all of a sudden, and the air became eerily still. This was probably a good time to tell you that we did not bring any bug spray. I think the entire mosquito nation descended upon us, and they knew we did not have any bug repellent. I am pretty sure I saw in the eyes of the bigger ones that they looked at us like we were lunch, and they were licking their stingers. There were so many of them that they blotted out the sun, and they looked like a big dark cloud surrounding us. They had their kamikaze group (or just the stupid ones) that landed on our arms and legs where they were easier to kill. The older stronger ones from the flock would land where you couldn't humanly reach them by yourself so they could land and just slurp up the sweet nectar of your blood that they were thirsting for. As we are trying to kill the pests that were landing on us, we were also trying to help each other out by slapping the ones on each other that could not be reached by the mosquito's current host. If someone had taken a video of this, I am guessing it would have been hilarious. There was a solid twenty minutes of slapping ourselves and each other. At one point, there was so much slapping going on that we all burst out laughing. There really wasn't anything funny about it because we were losing blood at an alarming rate to the evil cloud of the blood suckers. I imagine we each had to kill at least ten thousand of them fuckers. We were killing at least twenty of them with each slap. This was becoming a nightmare, and all we could hope for was that the mosquitos got full or that the river would pick up speed and get us out of there. The river finally picked up after about twenty minutes, and we arrived at our destination shortly thereafter. We were physically drained from all the slapping or the loss of blood; I'm not sure which one or maybe it was both. A very nice leisurely trip that started out awesome turned into a nightmare from hell. Fucking mosquitoes!

Hood Sledding

This is not a funny one but a little crazy and something I would never do with my kids. I am not a trophy-for-everyone or kneepad-and-helmets-when-leaving-the-house kind of dad, but I would not take my kids hood sledding. In Butte, Montana, where I grew up, there was a lake up in the mountains called Delmo Lake. It was up on top of the Continental Divide, so the elevation was roughly seven thousand feet above sea level. When you exited off the highway to head to the lake, there was a dirt road that was roughly six miles long to the lake. It was a winding road through the mountains, with trees on both sides of the road in spots and wide open fields that are like a marshland in some places. There were places with drop-offs that would not feel good if you went over the side. It was wide enough for cars to pass going in opposite direction in most places. My parents thought it would be a good idea in the wintertime to take an old fifties Chevy car hood, turn it upside down, tie a rope to the latch on the hood, tie the other end to the hitch on the truck, have us pile on, and head down that dirt road to the lake. Of course, there was no way to steer the hood or stop it if need be. It was common to come around a corner, and the hood full of people would be slung out into the marshland, and the hood would catch an edge and send us all flying. If you know anything about those old cars, you know how heavy the hoods were. If that hood would have caught one of us, it could have killed us easily. Sometimes we had to just bail off if the hood was headed for a tree. It was absolutely fucking crazy, but we all seemed to have a blast. I am not sure my dad wasn't trying to kill us.

From My Mom

This is the inscription my mom wrote in the Bible she gave me. It is very hard for me to read and even harder to write without tearing up. It is kind of in the opposite direction of what has been written in this book, but she was my best friend, and I miss her every day. So here goes:

> To my son Michael Jon,
> Of all the gifts you have ever or ever will receive, this is the greatest treasure by far that you could ever possess. For upon these pages lie the blueprints to life for both here and the hereafter. This book of life contains and supplies the answers to any and all questions that mankind could ever pose, for the author is the Creator of the universe and its entire contents, including every living creature. Once our life here has passed, only what's done for Christ will last. The troubles of this life will soon be over, but the joys to come will last forever. My deepest heartfelt prayer, my son, is that one day you

and I will walk on streets paved of gold. Should I go first, Michael, I will be waiting for you to join me. Remember, we have a final date to keep, just beyond the moon. I pray that as you read God's Word, you will grow in grace and knowledge and become closer to our blessed Savior daily. May God ever bless you, Michael, comfort, lead, guide, and control your life. Always walk close to him and you will find that every step you take he will take three. You will always prosper by putting Jesus first, loving him, serving him, and obeying him. He always hears and answers prayers, but since he knows the beginning and the end, he knows what's best for us. Sometimes he answers no or tells us to wait a while. If you remember this, you will never be disappointed or discouraged in God's answers to your prayers. Always keep your hand in the nail-scarred hand and be proud to be called a Christian, for you will never ever be called anything better in your entire lifetime. Always be honest, kind, and forgiving. Commit each day of your life to him anew, and he will always see you through. God loves you, Michael Jon, and so do I. I pray God's richest blessings upon you always. May God's love, peace, and the Holy Spirit's friendship ever be yours. Be strong, be happy, and grow in Christ. I love you with every fiber of my being, and I am so very proud that you are my son.

Love and prayers,
Mamma

I Wouldn't Touch Those

This one took place while I was working for a company called Areva. It was shortly after September, 11, 2001, so security was at an all-time high. It was fucking miserable. You got your ID and baggage checked at the ticket counter, checked again at the security check-point after you stripped down, and got a pat down on top of that. Of course, that was not enough because you had to also check in at your gate with your ticket and your ID. Even that was not enough. They had another table set up to "randomly" pull people out of the line at the gate check-in point to go through their carry-on again. You know how my luck goes. Yep, they "randomly" pull me out of line to check my ID, ticket, and carry-on bag. The guy in front of me was literally wearing a turban, and they randomly chose to check me instead of him? At this point, I should probably tell you that my daughter Marysa always put something in my bag so I would not forget her. One time, when I was in Hong Kong, I bought her this set of metal meditation balls that you rolled around in your hand, and they made a noise that was supposed to be therapeutic. They came in a little Chinese decorated box. Anyway, this particular trip, Marysa decided to put those in the backpack that I used as a carry-on.

So let's get back to the airport now. I got pulled out of line to get checked again. At this point, I was getting pissed. I got over to the little security tables, and she said she had to go through my bag. I asked her why she did not "randomly" pull the guy with the turban on his head out of line. I then asked her how many balding, fat middle-aged white guys were blowing shit up. She told me they couldn't profile. I told her that was the fucking problem right there. So instead of profiling and maybe catching someone with a bomb, they would rather swing hard the other way to prove that they were not profiling by pulling people like me out of line to check their bags. I think they lost focus of the goal. That was like taking a shit and wiping your nose when you were done instead of wiping your ass. That was just fucking stupid. She started digging through my bag and came across the therapeutic balls I was talking about earlier. She opened the box and pulled one of the balls out of the box, and it made a little noise. She held it up above her and looked at it in the light. She picked up the other one and was kind of moving them around in her hand, and it hit me. I told her, "I wouldn't be handling them if I were you, and you should probably wash your hands when you are done with them."

She looked at me curiously and asked me why. I told her because I had them in my ass this morning and hadn't had a chance to wash them. The people behind me broke out into deep belly laughter, and it pissed her off. She put them back in the box, put the box back in my bag, and with a very disgusted look, pushed my bag back across the table to me and said, "You can go."

I said, "Thanks and maybe you should be profiling." I laughed. She didn't.

Crackhead

We went down to my nephew's house for the Fourth of July to visit and hang out at their new pool. We had a really good time catching up and sharing a little moonshine. As we were talking and drinking, we decided to head to the nearest strip mall to catch a fireworks show. We arrived at the strip mall and found a parking space. We all piled out and set up chairs on the nearby strip of grass. We also laid out a couple of blankets and passed around the moonshine. The kids decided they needed something to drink. I gave them money, and off to the nearby store they went. After about thirty minutes, I noticed the kids were not back from getting drinks. I went looking for them, and when I got to the other side of the parking lot, I noticed this guy, around thirty years old, just sitting in the back of his truck by himself. Not so funny, if that was where the encounter was to end. The sun was setting, so it was starting to get dark. All I could see was his head, like it was floating in the air, or maybe he was hiding from someone. I chuckled because those thoughts ran through my head. I could see the headline now: "Man Encounters Floating Head in Back of Pickup Truck." Then I heard him yelling at me, "What is that?" And he pointed to the sky. I tried to ignore him, but he was persistent. So I looked, and what I saw was amazing; it was an airplane. I told him it was an airplane. He didn't believe me, and by this time, all I could see was his forehead and eyes. He said it was not flying straight and was going too slow to be an airplane. He then popped his whole head up out of the back of the truck and smiled at me like I was the dumb one. I could see he was messed up pretty bad and that he believed what he saw was real. He was all disheveled like the last rose of summer and was missing all his front teeth. I told him it was flying straight and that he should put down the crack pipe and see a dentist.

Fuck Me

Here is a short one that's not funny, but it did piss me off. Okay, it may be funny to you. I was in the shower minding my own business. No, I was not snapping my carrot, and I grabbed the bodywash off the shelf. No big deal, right? Wrong! As I lowered the bodywash bottle to the sponge to distribute the appropriate amount of soap onto the sponge, I hit the single handle lever for the hot and cold water and changed the temperature of the water from warm to hotter that the fucking sun. I could tell what the temperature was because, of course, the water was spraying directly onto my junk. If I could think of a temp hotter than the sun, that was what I would have written down. I got the water turned down before it did any damage and I needed a skin graph. That was the very area I was hoping to use for a skin graph should I ever need one. So after all the excitement was over and the water temp was fine and my balls were not like chestnuts roasting on an open fire, I still needed to proceed with my shower and the fundamentals of ensuring I did a thorough job of cleaning myself. I reached for the bodywash, after stepping to the back of the shower as far away as possible from the lever from hell, snapped the cap open, and poured it directly onto the sponge. As I snapped the cap closed, it shot a laser of soap directly at my pupil. Not even grazing an eyelid or eyelash but direct hit at the center of the pupil. It burned like someone lit a match and threw it into my eye. I think maybe I need to start taking baths.

Haircut

I took the kids to get a haircut the other day to a place called Great Clips. Great, my ass! We walked in and took a seat while we were waiting for someone to come to the counter. I thought she was going to just ask for our names, so I did not get out of my chair, as we were just a few feet away from the counter. So I told her our names, and then she asked for our address, home phone, cell phone, and work phone. I just kept yelling out the information to her, and for some reason, it got funnier the more information she asked for, the more I shouted out the answers. When I had completed my transfer of information task, she started on another guy for information. He started shouting out his information, and we all just lost it and started laughing out loud because he was a lot farther away from the counter. Maybe you had to be there, but it was hilarious. Next thing that happened was a guy came from the back after a fresh haircut and bellied up to the counter to pay his bill. Now his back was to us, and we could see this clump of hair on the back of his neck that was missed by the girl who cut his hair. I was not sure how she missed it, as there was enough hair in that patch of turf she left to make a small bird's nest. We laughed because that was what we do. Marysa looked at me all scared, with eyes big and wide open, and said, "I don't want her to cut my hair."

That same girl came to the counter and called out another lady's name, so Marysa let out a sigh of relief. Unlucky as we were that girl (The Butcher) did not know how to cut that lady's hair, so she came out to the counter to call on her next victim. That lucky customer was Marysa. Marysa looked at me just horrified but got up to go let this girl cut her hair. I could not let that happen, so I said I would go first so Marysa would get someone else to cut her hair. It was a good thing I stepped in for Marysa because this poor girl had no idea how to cut hair. I told her to put a number 1 guard on and cut it all the same length and just square the back. After her fist attempt, she asked me if it was okay. I said, "No, you missed here and here and here."

We went through this same drill three fucking times before this inept thing got it to a satisfactory level. I could have cut my own hair better. She did not get a tip, and she should really think about a different career because she has no business cutting hair.

Rudolph

It was Christmas Eve, and we were sitting at the table eating crab legs, clams, and shrimp scampi like we did every year. We were at the table, just having a normal conversation, and Zaq looked up from the table, pointed at this big zit on Marysa's nose, and said, "Does Santa know you will be guiding his sleigh tonight?"

It was so funny because it came out of nowhere.

Air Travel

On one of many trips taken by plane, and this happened often, I got to sit right next to what appeared to be a chatty Kathy Doll with a three hundred feet pull string pulled to the extreme end of the chord. Just talk, talk, talk, talk, until it was just unbearable and you couldn't take anymore so you put on your headphones to drop a subtle hint to shut the fuck up. The exaggeration of me grabbing my headphones, holding them out in front of me like I was inspecting them for damage, and pulling them wide open to place on my head did not stop this particular Kathy. His string was pulled to the end, and by God, he was going to get the words out whether I liked it or not. The only thing I remember him talking about was his kids, and when he asked if I wanted to see a picture of his kids, I said, "No, thank you." And he showed me anyway. I guess that might make me an asshole in some people's eyes, but I didn't give two shits about seeing pictures of people I would never see or know. It was bad enough that now I knew there were going to be three more little bastards out there in the world that would be on airplanes boring people who they didn't know to death with their life stories. Not to mention they would not be taught the art of subtle hint awareness. Maybe there is something wrong with me, but I just don't like people that much. The older I get, the more I just want my family around me.

One Eye

Here is just a thought I had and decided I would share with you. Earlier, I wrote about a family that had a father, a son, and a dog with only one working eye. As I thought back to my childhood, I realized there were a number of people who I crossed paths with who were visually challenged. I also had a cousin with only one working eye. I also had a one-eyed shop teacher in school who was bald and also missing a couple of digits. Our local butcher Bill was sporting just one eye that had sight and the other one just kind of had a slimy glaze covering it. He was also missing a couple of fingers. I am sure there were others. I am beginning to wonder if we should change the name of the town to Cyclopsville.

Julie's People

This is a story I wish someone had recorded, but they didn't, so there is no use crying about it now. I will try to capture what was said, but I am sure it won't do it justice because you had to be there. I believe it is still a story worth sharing, so here goes.

One summer, my brother Doug; his wife, Julie; my cousin Donna; and her husband, Jim; and I went to a place called Silverwood in Northern Idaho. We went there to visit an amusement park and stayed there for the weekend. We were in the hotel bar having a few adult beverages, and Julie started talking about her childhood and some of the people who were in her life. The sad part was I couldn't remember the stories or anecdotes I was coming up with as she rattled off another name in her childhood gang of thieves. Everyone was in tears laughing at what I was saying, but I was a little drunk, so I couldn't remember what I was saying, as it was a long time ago. You will understand when I tell you their names. Eldo Sunnysack was the first name she threw out there, and just hearing that name, you know I had to jump on it. The name alone was funny, but when you hear that he got caught fucking a horse, it was hilarious and made sense. It was probably not funny to the horse or the owner of the horse. I heard she was still pissed about the local livestock rapist getting a turn with her horse. His nickname in school was Dildo Gunnysack. I don't care who you are. That's funny unless you are brain dead.

So after the laughter died down, I asked her to keep going with stories about her gang of little rascals. Next name out of the shoots was Bucky Fountain. She swore these were real names. I can't remember what I said about him, but he does have a sister named Ladawna Quimby Fountain. Now you know how cruel kids are, and with names like these, I am sure there was no shortage of getting teased.

Next person to get unmasked was ole One Nut Larry. Larry shot off one of his own nuts with a shotgun. He said he was climbing a fence, and the gun just went off. From the sound of the other stories, I think Larry might be lying, but we would never know. Maybe he could catch up with ole Eldo Sunnysack, and they could go cow tipping. Wink, wink.

The Love Story

Here is another one that is not mine, but I found it very funny. I will set the scene for you. It was kind of like a fart in church. Outside, on the playground, or in a bar, it was no big deal. Let one bounce off a pew so everyone could hear it during a sermon, and the laughter would be too great to hold in. My boss hired this new engineer into our group, and her name was Rachel Love. You need to remember her last name for the rest of this story. She was telling us how, at her last job, she worked with a bunch of stuffy engineers that never joked around or laughed, ever. That sounded about right when it came to engineers. So there were a bunch of engineers from her office that went on the road to an outage at a nuclear plant. They were sharing a small space with the customer during the outage, and it was kind of an open forum, so everyone could hear what you were saying if they wanted to. Rachel started telling this story about how her sister was getting married to a guy with the last name of Swallow. Her sister did not want it in the paper because the announcement would read "Love to Swallow will be sharing vows on June 16." None of the engineers laughed, but the customer did, and I was laughing my ass off. That was funny shit, and to top it off, her soon-to-be husband had a brother named William Jason Swallow, and they called him Will. So he signed shit with "Will Jason Swallow." Good stuff.

Coffee

At work, I had an office right across from a little kitchen that everyone in the building used. I went in there every morning to get water and ice. One morning, it hit me funny that every time I went in there, someone was bitching about having to make coffee. I guess because they had not had any coffee yet that morning. I didn't know what that was like because I didn't drink coffee. I was glad they were freaking out for a cup of coffee, and there was none because it started my day out with a laugh. I wrote down some of the things they said when there was no coffee made or someone left them half of a cup.

- This is fucking bullshit.
- What the fuck? Who leaves half a cup of coffee? (A person with a full cup.)
- Son of a bitch, I think I am the only one that makes coffee in this whole fucking building.
- I can't stand a motherfucker that won't make a pot of coffee.
- They need to put a camera in here and find out who is taking the last cup of coffee and not making another pot and fire the son of a bitch.
- I am going to kill someone.

- I am going to find that fucker and shove this empty pot up his ass.
- Shit!
- I work with a bunch of lazy assholes. How hard is it to make a fucking pot of coffee?
- Why? Why? Why would you take the last cup and walk away without making more? I hope your mom gets cancer, you rotten bastard.

Fish Tank

Here is another WTF. Just the other day, I decided it was time to clean my fish tank. It was not a huge tank; only fifty-five gallons was all she would hold. I asked Marysa to help me by dumping the buckets of water as I vacuumed the water and fish shit out of the tank and into the buckets. We were using a five-gallon bucket, and when it was about full, we noticed it had leaked all over the floor. She ran it to the door, leaving a trail of water all the way to the door. No big deal, mop it up, and get another bucket. Of course, I was standing there the whole time, waiting on her with my thumb over the end of the hose so I didn't lose the suction I had. She finally found a two-gallon mop bucket and moseyed back to the fish tank to finish our task. It turned out this bucket had an even bigger crack in it, and she lost most of the water on the way to the door. Yet another trail of shitty fish water to clean up. Fuck me! So now she grabbed a kitchen garbage can and brought it to the scene of the crime. I asked her if she checked this one for holes. She said she did check it, so I started filling up the can. We got about halfway, and when she picked up the can, it just started pouring out of it. It turned out that half of the bottom of the can had a crack in it, so when she picked it up, it just opened up the crack like there was no bottom at all. I could have just siphoned all the water onto the floor and cleaned it up. That would have been a little less frustrating. We finally found a five-gallon bucket with no holes or cracks and completed the task at hand.

Hillbilly Christmas Dinner

This one started with a girl I was dating, who lived in a very small town. It was the kind of town with a train stop and a general store. There was one road going through town with one cross road. I was surprised the streets were paved. This little town did not even have a blinking yellow caution light at the one intersection in town. There were a couple of houses, but the population couldn't have been more than a couple hundred. She asked me if I wanted to go to dinner at her family's house, so I said sure. It was a Saturday night, and we headed to the thriving metropolis. As we were getting deeper off the beaten path, I was starting to get a little nervous, so I looked at her and asked if "I" was going to be dinner.

She laughed and said, "No, don't be stupid."

I then told her, "If I hear banjo music, I am fucking out of there." I didn't hear any banjo music, so we kept driving.

We arrived at the house, got out of the car, and walked in the back door. They welcomed me with open arms, and the first person I met was Fred, whom they called Little John. He talked exactly like Boomhauer on *King of the Hill*. I could not understand a single word he said, so I just looked at her and raised my eyebrows like "WTF." She just laughed and hit me in the arm. The next person I met was Joe. He was a very nice, normal guy. Then on to Kathy, who was forty, and her husband, Eddy, who was sixty-seven. Up next was Fred's wife, Anita. My girl's sister, Woodchuck, and her husband, Lilwayne. And no party was complete without the lady from across the street named Julie.

By the way everyone was acting. It was apparent they did not wait for us before they broke into the whiskey-soaked eggnog. So we got a drink and joined in the conversations and partook in a couple of hors d'oeuvres. About an hour later, we sat down to dinner at a table for six. In case you weren't keeping track, the head count was at ten. So it was a little cozy, to say the least. The food was great, and the liquor was flowing like wine. The conversation was good, and I was having a great time. These were really nice people. Everyone was wondering why Joe did not bring the fireworks this year. I guess he put on quite a show every year. This year, he only brought sparklers. We were going to go outside and light some sparklers but decided to down some moonshine before we kicked off those particular activities.

After a few more rounds of moonshine, Joe broke out the sparklers. The centerpiece on the table was a wreath with five candles burning in it. He started passing out sparklers to everyone. I declined the offer because Joe, in his infinite wisdom, thought it would be a good idea to light the sparklers inside the house. Joe informed everyone that the only thing we had to be careful with was the tablecloth because it was a family heirloom. I was thinking there might be a few other items sitting around that might need to be avoided, along with the tablecloth. Like maybe all the liquor and the moonshine, not to mention the drapes in this cramped space where we were all sitting. Everyone who was handed a sparkler started lighting them from the candles on the centerpiece. Everything was good at first, and then the fun began. The first thing that happened was the tablecloth caught fire, and then a napkin on the tablecloth was on fire. They put out the fire on the tablecloth and took the napkin that was on fire and threw it on the floor, which was carpeted, so now the carpet was on fire. They stomped out the fire on the carpet, and the excitement died down for a minute. While they were inspecting the hole the fire burned in the tablecloth, someone spilled a glass of red wine on the tablecloth. The only thing they didn't do to the heirloom tablecloth was wipe their ass on it. That poor tablecloth was torn up three ways to Sunday. It didn't seem to bother them too much because they were all laughing, but that might have been the moonshine talking. I am sure they felt a little different the next day when they were sober. That poor fucking tablecloth took a good old-fashioned ass beating. While we were examining the hole that was burned in the carpet, someone said they had a rainbow vacuum that could fix the hole.

I told her, "I didn't know a vacuum could fix holes in a carpet. Does it give blowjobs as well?"

That comment brought on a round of laughter. After that died down, they started talking about lighting real candles that were hanging on the Christmas tree. At that point, I was planning my escape route for when they actually burned the house to the ground. With some persuading, they decided not to light the candles on the tree. I was glad to see they came to their senses.

Then they started talking about good ole cousin Charles. He had one regular arm and hand. They told me he had one little T-rex arm and hand. Apparently, he walked with a limp because one leg was shorter than the other, so he just dragged the short leg around. He cut Joe's grass for ten dollars. Apparently, as the story goes, Charles had a brother that spent his disability check, which pissed off Charles. Charles had to hide his checkbook from his brother and his brother's wife so they wouldn't spend all his money. Charles liked to drink a lot and walked everywhere. Did I mention he couldn't read or write? Poor fucker couldn't catch a break.

The next story I heard was about the person they called The Lawnmower Man. This tiny town was starting to shape up as comedy gold. He rode around town all day, looking for lawns to mow. Sounds harmless and uneventful, right? Here's the catch. The riding lawnmower did not have blades on it, so he rigged a push mower up to the riding mower. He dragged the push mower around with him, and when he got a job, he fired up the push mower and dragged it around the yard with the riding mower. I would love to see that in person.

The next story was about a man lady by the last name of Perry. Apparently, she was a fighter, and I was informed that if she came at me, I was supposed to beat her down like a man. If I didn't, they informed me that she would kick my ass. I assured them that if we crossed paths and she came at me, I would club her like a baby seal.

The next story was about her three sons that the town referred to as the Perry brothers. I guess they were hellions, and one night, they got all liquored up and were driving all over the county causing hate and discontent. Finally, the sheriff pulled them over and asked them what they were doing and if they had been drinking. The sheriff shone his flashlight in the truck, and all three of them were sitting in the front seat. He shone his flashlight on the brother in the middle and asked the other two what was wrong with their brother. They said there was nothing wrong with him and that he was just drunk. Come to find out, he had been dead for hours at that point.

At this point, I had to piss and wondered what other crazy shit I would encounter. I asked and they told me where the bathroom was, so off I went, past the burnt tablecloth and stepped over the hole that was burned in the carpet to arrive at the bathroom door. As I entered the bathroom, I noticed a note balanced on the hot water faucet handle that said, "Do not use." I looked down, and I saw there was no drain line coming from the sink, but there was a bucket that caught everything that found its way down the sink drain. So I was standing there pissing, and the wall behind the toilet was tiled with four-inch square white tiles. Not a big deal until I noticed there were four tiles hanging out of place. They were about two inches out of place and were hung there with Scotch tape two inches below their assigned space on the wall, hanging there like a Christmas tree ornament.

I had quite the night of laughter listening to the stories of that little town.

Stan

This is about a guy I worked with called Stan. You may have guessed that by the title of this little story. I will describe Stan's physical features and then tell the rest of the story. Just so we are all clear, Stan is a great guy and would have laughed if he had been in the room. He is about 5 feet, 7 inches tall and tips the scales at roughly 230 pounds, I am guessing. He has short legs and a big, tight belly. He kind of looks like he is riding a chicken. He is always wearing button-up shirts that are pulled over his belly tighter than the skin on a hotdog and tucked into his pants. I was talking to a couple of other coworkers who had asked me if I had seen Stan today. I informed them that I had seen Stan and that it was dangerous because I did not have on safety glasses or a face shield. They asked me why I would need to deploy visual safety devices, and I told them because Stan wore his shirts so tight that I was scared one of the buttons would pop off and put my eye out. I went on to say if he wore his pants that tight, the whole world would know if he was circumcised. They were laughing pretty hard, and I said we may need a job safety analysis to have a meeting in the same room with him.

Bathroom Barber

Lately, at work, it seemed like every time I went into the bathroom, I would find clumps of hair on the toilet seat. That was just fucking nasty, and I swore that if I found out who the bathroom barber was, I was going to dip him in a tank of Nair hair removal. The hair was all over the urinal and the shitters alike. It was like someone was shaving their junk every time they went in the bathroom. If I were collecting the hair, I would have enough to weave an Indian blanket. Nasty.

Buttered Popcorn Piss

The other day at work, I went walking into the bathroom, and as I opened the door, I was greeted with what could only be described as wholly fucking shit. The smell was just horrible. I thought to myself, *Is someone gutting a moose?* I had to piss really bad, so I trudged into the bathroom and bellied up to the urinal to take a piss. As I was pissing, I noticed that my piss smelled like hot buttered popcorn from the movie theater, which gave me some relief from Sir Shits-a-Lot's nasty ass. I didn't even want to know what he had been eating if it made his shit smell like that.

Duck versus Dick

I was in a meeting the other day, and I guess there were about six of us in the room. The mix was two ladies and four guys. The two ladies were helping us with the changes we were making to our processes at work. They were very helpful. They were not outage people.

That meant they did not go on outages at the nuclear plants like the rest of us did. Sometimes when we got into discussions about outages, they just did their own thing until we got back on track. We were always laughing about something. It was a great group to work with and really was a lot of fun.

One of the ladies had her desktop up on the big screen because we were revising a form, and she was making the corrections for us. That way, we could all see what she was doing while making the corrections real time. A couple of us got off on a tangent, and I guess she got bored and forgot that we could all see everything she was doing on her computer because it was up on the big screen in the conference room. So she decided to send an instant message to the other lady in the room, which was no big deal, except that in this case, we could see what she had typed. The instant message said, "I like dicks. Do you like dicks?"

Just as I looked at the screen and saw what she typed, she also realized it and turned beet red. I asked the other lady if she was going to answer. We all laughed so hard we were crying. What she meant to type was *ducks*, not *dicks*. Finally, we all calmed down and got back to work. A little later, I had to use the bathroom, and when I got back into the room, I told them I had to apologize for taking so long, but I stepped on my duck and sprained my ankle. Laughter erupted again. It was a good day.

Here are some of my Facebook rants. People seemed to like them, so I thought I would share some with you.

Politician

I was thinking we should change the meaning of a certain word in the dictionary. That word is *politician*. We should change the meaning of that word to read the following: politician—lying, no good pieces of shit that no one can trust.

Trip from Pasco

I had a trip from hell from Pasco, Washington, yesterday that lasted into today. Not that anyone gives a shit, but I thought I would write it down anyway. I am sure you all have had trips like this before.

Up at 0530 to have meetings all day.

Leave Pasco at 1930.

Arrive Seattle at 2030.

Leave Seattle late at 2230.

Plan on sleeping on the five-hour flight to Charlotte.

A baby cried for four and a half hours of the trip (motherfucker); not one ounce of shut-eye was had by me or anyone.

Someone was farting the whole five-hour flight. Not just a whiff and what-was-that. I am talking trucker-eating-chili-and-broccoli farts that would gag a maggot off a shitwagon and maybe even cause a tear or two.

Arrive late to Charlotte, tired as fuck.

Run to the next gate to get to Lynchburg and thought I would not make it because it was at the other end of the airport. Get to the gate and the flight was delayed. It was now 0730.

Finally, board at 0745 and take off. It was supposed to be a forty-five-minute flight. After circling the Lynchburg airport for one and a half hours because of fog, we landed in Roanoke and were being told we were being bussed to Lynchburg.

Not happening; so we rented a car and drove to Lynchburg. Fuck me. Hungry as fuck, I stopped at Taco Bell (my Graceland) to get something to eat. I ordered and received my food. As always, I filled my cup with Baja Blast and couldn't wait to drink it. I inserted the straw and tried to take a drink, but nothing happened. That cool, sweet liquid did not make it to my lips no matter how hard I sucked. The straw was melted shut on the end I inserted into the cup. Will this trip ever stop sucking?

Canadian KFC

I wrote this while I was in Canada for my job. Let me tell you a story about the fucked-up KFC here in Canada. I stopped by the KFC to get some chicken. No big deal, right? Well, it was, because when I asked for a breast and a wing, they said, "We don't have any breasts, but we have wings."

So I said, "Give me four wings then, please." That was when they told me they only had one wing. I was, like, *WTF.* So I asked for a cheeseburger. They told me that they didn't sell cheeseburgers. I said, "Apparently, you don't sell fucking chicken either, and I was just exploring my options."

The people in line behind me started laughing and walking out because they didn't have any chicken. I tried again another night to get that ever-elusive chicken breast at the KFC. My quest was thwarted yet again by the KFC not having any chicken. To be fair, they did have thighs, but who the fuck wanted a thigh from the KFC. I asked for a breast, and they said they were fresh out. I asked for wings, and again, I got a "Sorry, we are fresh out."

"How about a chicken sandwich?"

"Nope, no chicken sandwich."

I then asked for some ribs, and they said they didn't sell ribs. Again, I said, "You don't sell chicken either." I then asked them why they were open if they didn't have any chicken.

They said they had some earlier. I said, "Earlier? Its six o'fucking-clock. I could see if it was midnight." I told him he might want to think about selling pizza since there seemed to be a chicken shortage in Canada. I ended up just buying a soda, and when I went to the drink machine, it was absolutely disgusting. The drain bin looked like a slimy pond, and just to piss me off further, there was no ice. I guess the chicken must have run off with all the ice. I filled my cup up anyway because I had already paid for it and didn't want to tax the brain of the poor counter guy. I then went on the hunt for a straw, and guess what, you got it, no fucking straws. They were fresh out of straws. To top it off, a guy came from the kitchen looking like Kramer from *Seinfeld*, with shorter hair. He was all knock-kneed and covered in flour that must have been from some other day when they actually had chicken. He weighed about a buck twenty-five and had a size 15 shoe. He looked like he had clown shoes on. I left, never to return. Can you believe a fucking chicken place with no chicken? WTF!

Hollywood

Anyone else sick and tired of all the award shows that Hollywood bestows upon themselves? Look at me, I'm pretty, I'm rich, and I'm getting another award for pretending to be someone I am not. I don't even know how many of these award ceremonies they have for each other. All I know is it is way too many. I hate them all.

Toilet Paper

I was in the store the other day and went down the toilet paper aisle, and the shelves were empty due to the COVID-19 pandemic. I went about my business shopping and happened by the cheese aisle, and that was when it hit me. No toilet paper, but there was plenty of cheese! If you eat enough cheese, you won't need toilet paper. So if you are out of toilet paper, get you some of nature's lock tight and forget about all your dirty-ass worries. Or you can just shit in the shower and waffle stomp that shit down the drain.

The following is something someone wrote down as I was having a meeting, and then he just started writing shit down that I said. Not sure why he did this, but he sent it to me, and the results are below. He was the one who named it.

Webster's Quotable Quotes

1. You don't want to be in the shithole we were in.
2. Yeah right, get fucked.
3. Look! A bipolar Crelican movement. That's rare.
4. I don't know how the hell you'll fix that.
5. We put that short arm in, and it was rock and roll!
6. We're tracking it. We just can't find it.
7. Eight welds in eight days—somebody's smoking crack.
8. Shut the fuck up.
9. Love you. Mean it.
10. Roll over, bitch.
11. Bryce, what are you doing?
12. I moved into your office. Nobody told ya? Well, cat's outta the bag.
13. See if you can read this. Nah, it's too small. I need glasses.
14. Don't get divorced in Virginia. Either move to another state or kill her.
15. Oh my god! You shipped contaminated equipment to a nuclear plant? That's like shipping hops to a brewery.
16. He's a real cock head.
17. Tell them to put a rubber band around their head and snap the hell out of it.

18. Hey, buckwheat! We don't have nightshift. It's midnight, and I'm drunk.
19. A 3 on the survey? Did you kick somebody in the balls or what?
20. What the fuck is a 3 on a survey? A babbling idiot or a complete loser?
21. We put some kind of thing in that measures volts. A voltmeter? Duh. No.
22. There was just so much shit going into the pot.
23. When you're going down in the annulus, it's already tight.
24. You might as well write them on a bar napkin with a crayon. That's how good they are.
25. You ask them for what's in the SRD, and you get an ice house from Minnesota.
26. Those handicap porta-johns are cool. You slap your laptop down, flip the sign to "Occupied," and turn on the porn; and you're good to go.
27. Some people don't like them, but they're idiots.
28. They were so far up your ass with a borescope that they could see the roof of your mouth.
29. Smells like rubber band time.
30. The safest place is to be on schedule. (No kidding, that's a real DC Cook entrance sign about four feet wide.)
31. It's geometry. It'll go away. Watch, see? I turned my scope off, and they went away.
32. He couldn't say shit if his mouth was full of it.
33. Oh, fuck a bunch of that.
34. That would have been an outstanding place to throw him a rubber band.
35. They didn't want us to come on-site and steal their technology. Yeah right. I'll do that right after I steal your ugly sister.
36. We'll get one of 'em. They will fall on their nuts.
37. You need to sit here. No shit, Jojo.
38. It's like working on a pig farm and saying, "Don't get any pig shit on your shoe."

39. That's gonna feel better when it quits hurtin'.
40. Put a catcher's mitt on your REL for when they drop that dummy sleeve.
41. You say tomato; I say fuck off.
42. I'd rather have somebody step on my balls with golf shoes on.

Big Daddy Mike ⎁ grew up in a small mining town in Butte, Montana. He loved his childhood there and wouldn't change it for the world. He decided to write this book because of all the things he would say and write down. He had all the people around him tell him he should write a book, so he did. He has not published any other books and was hesitant to try and publish this book because he wasn't sure people wanted to hear what he had to say. He spent ten years in the Navy as a welder and Nondestructive Examination Inspector. When he left the Navy, he spent eight years at GE as an inspector until he left there to work at another nuclear company called Framatome. He makes his home in Virginia now but gets home to Montana whenever he can.